T5-DHH-681

SPECIAL MESSAGE TO READERS

This book is published under the auspices of

THE ULVERSCROFT FOUNDATION

(registered charity No. 264873 UK)

Established in 1972 to provide funds for research, diagnosis and treatment of eye diseases. Examples of contributions made are: —

A Children's Assessment Unit at Moorfield's Hospital, London.

•

Twin operating theatres at the Western Ophthalmic Hospital, London.

•

A Chair of Ophthalmology at the Royal Australian College of Ophthalmologists.

•

The Ulverscroft Children's Eye Unit at the Great Ormond Street Hospital For Sick Children, London.

You can help further the work of the Foundation by making a donation or leaving a legacy. Every contribution, no matter how small, is received with gratitude. Please write for details to:

**THE ULVERSCROFT FOUNDATION,
The Green, Bradgate Road, Anstey,
Leicester LE7 7FU, England.
Telephone: (0116) 236 4325**

**In Australia write to:
THE ULVERSCROFT FOUNDATION,
c/o The Royal Australian College of
Ophthalmologists,
27, Commonwealth Street, Sydney,
N.S.W. 2010.**

DEATH OF A DOCTOR

When Dr Carleton Spence was discovered dead in his study, savagely stabbed, Inspector Bob Channing had to find a suspect. But that wasn't as easy as it should have been, because it seemed that everybody disliked Carleton Spence. Although Inspector Channing was finally able to disclose the murderer's identity, and the ingenious manner in which the doctor had been killed, he was never able to arrest his suspect.

Books by John Armour
in the Linford Mystery Library:

MURDER IN HAWTHORN

JOHN ARMOUR

DEATH OF A DOCTOR

Complete and Unabridged

LINFORD
Leicester

First published in Great Britain in 1969 by
Robert Hale & Company
London

First Linford Edition
published 2000
by arrangement with
Robert Hale Limited
London

Copyright © 1969 by Robert Hale & Company
All rights reserved

British Library CIP Data

Armour, John, *1916*–
    Death of a doctor.—Large print ed.—
Linford mystery library
    1. Detective and mystery stories
    2. Large type books
    I. Title
    823.9'14 [F]

ISBN 0–7089–5718–8

Published by
F. A. Thorpe (Publishing) Ltd.
Anstey, Leicestershire

Set by Words & Graphics Ltd.
Anstey, Leicestershire
Printed and bound in Great Britain by
T. J. International Ltd., Padstow, Cornwall

This book is printed on acid-free paper

1

Doctor Carleton Spence

A discernible fact of life is that certain professions endow their practitioners with specific mannerisms, even specific personalities, providing of course they did not already have strong personalities before coming under the spell of their vocations.

Doctor Carleton Spence was every inch the medical man. He was calm, sedate, quietly immersed in his work, tall, grey and very dignified. He had been described as a great stuffed-shirt, as an angel of mercy, as a pompous charlatan and as a surgical wizard.

To tread safe ground it might have been fairer to seek a true description somewhere between the extremes, but Doctor Spence was that rare exception to the rule — he *was* a pompous charlatan. He shared that unique distinction with perhaps half the practitioners of his art, but such has been the contrived image of physicians and surgeons that generally speaking, they are viewed as intellectual giants whose expensive training has endowed them with something akin to godliness.

Far be it from any practising physician to mar that image, and for this at least practical people cannot blame them, although for their science, good as it is and getting better constantly, not one out of twenty is actually fit.

It has been the deference, doubtless, that has affected them most; there are few physicians who are not constantly aware that they can save lives. Whether they save more than they lose is not the issue. It would be difficult for any man not to act differently under the lasting aura of superiority with which mankind has surrounded doctors.

If the doctor already had a high opinion of himself, it could be reasonably expected that this aura would most certainly enhance it.

Doctor Carleton Spence, for example,

wore a corset. He also wore his thick mane of grey hair long and well combed, especially on the sides where it had been trained into aristocratic waves. He made a point of always listening to whatever was being said as though he'd heard it all before and was being courteous to listen again.

He was worth a lot of money. After all, one didn't come endowed with a great ego to a profession that sustained that ego unwaveringly, without developing a splendid capacity for entering a sick-room as though arriving directly from Heaven, and afterwards charging fees as though they were based upon the mileage.

He was a widower of some twenty years, which helped enormously when a patient was a woman, preferably of middle, or later, age.

His face was pale, beefy, with the small, thick-lipped mouth, the thinnish, beaked little nose, and the pale eyes, all pushed up into the centre of it. When elderly widows found Doctor Spence handsome it had to mean they found him distinguished-looking because his features, his eyes and mouth, were far from prepossessing. But in total, the carefully waved way he combed his heavy mane of grey hair, his somewhat formidable bulk, his air of great and quiet wisdom, cultivated until he could no longer separate his real self from his affected self, made him seem handsome. Not in a sexy way of course, it was improbable that ailing elderly women had any urges in that direction, but rather, handsome in a god-figure and father-figure way, both combined.

Doctor William Linden, with whom Doctor Spence co-operated at the clinic owned by the former and managed by the latter, had once in an annoyed or unguarded moment, called Doctor Spence 'the reason elderly widows get sick, illness aside.'

Doctor Linden was a mild, thoughtful, youngish man. It would be difficult after knowing him, to imagine him down-grading anyone, and for him to make a remark such as the one he'd made about Carleton Spence, he would have had to have been very annoyed.

But Carter Spence, nephew to Carleton Spence, was a different variety of person. He'd spent eight years in the army and ten years after that in construction. He was as big as his uncle but without an ounce of fat on his frame, and he had a tanned, square face showing no softness anywhere. He'd come to manhood in a rough environment and had afterwards moved into a tough one. He was rough himself, sometimes crude, and one could expect quick, direct, candid appraisals from him.

When Doctor Spence summoned him and made the offer of manager of Doctor Spence's real estate holdings Carter Spence had laughed in his face.

'Uncle,' he'd said, 'I can stand a man who beats his wife, even a guy who smokes in bed and loafs on the job a damned sight better than I can stand a phony. And that's exactly what you are in my opinion — a twenty-four carat gold phony.'

Doctor Spence hadn't got over that for six months, during which time he hired an aging widower named Ford to manage his rentals, and his nephew had gone off to British Columbia on a construction undertaking of awesome magnitude — the erection of a city in a muskeg swamp.

It was during the second half of that ensuing year that Doctor Spence, who had braved all the emotional assaults of widows and others for twenty years, fell before the blandishments of a forty-year-old unmarried woman named Maude Engels.

They were married in Lebanon, Ohio, went to Moscow, Idaho, for a two weeks' honeymoon, then, deciding Idaho's outback was a bit much, flew to Florida and spent the next two weeks on the Gold Coast where culture and civilisation surrounded them completely.

After that, they returned to Los Angeles — the suburb of Santa Monica actually — where Doctor Spence had his practice, his holdings, and his very elegant Moorish-type hilltop home overlooking the Pacific Ocean.

Janie Ford, daughter of the manager of the Spence properties summed up Maude

Spence in two words. 'Very efficient.' Upon reflection one would have been entitled to wonder if Janie had meant that in all the varied ways it could have been interpreted. For example, did she mean Maude was efficient at calculating how to marry a very wealthy doctor? Did she mean Maude was efficient at running, organizing, moderating the doctor's life? And did she by any chance also mean that Maude, a very strikingly handsome woman at forty, knew precisely what she wanted from life, and had she cold-bloodedly and efficiently gone about getting it?

On the charitable side, Maude Spence was an asset. She dressed very well, always looked as though she'd just stepped forth from either a band-box or a beauty parlour, or perhaps both simultaneously, and her large, stone-steady grey eyes complimented a strong, smooth, aristocratic set of handsome features. She was one of those women people turned to gaze back at. Not just men, but women also.

Oddly enough, men, while willing to

concede that Maude was a beautiful woman, were evidently not drawn to her for the usual reasons even though she was high-breasted, firm-hipped, and possessed amazingly supple and muscular legs. Carter Spence would have occasion to tell quiet and thoughtful Detective Inspector Robert Channing that Maude Engels-Spence was a damned well built block of blue ice, perhaps an apt enough description, and most certainly one that only Carter Spence could have conjured up.

Maude affected an air of quiet, unshakable and utterly serene superiority on the one hand, and on the other hand she dismissed all Doctor Spence's servants except Mary Martin, the maid, and prepared all the meals herself, which was a little out of character, or so it seemed at least, for when one saw Maude in stores or at bridge parties, she was every inch the *grande dame*, although a bit young for that projection.

There was no way to actually or accurately judge what life was like behind the soaring white walls of the Moorish residence atop its beautifully landscaped Santa Monica knoll where the doctor, his lady, and their one servant, lived. But if outward appearances meant anything at all, no great changes had taken place. The doctor still emerged, corseted, combed, talced, and each morning drove his white Lincoln Continental to the clinic, impassive, pale and overweight as ever, and usually several hours later, handsome Maude emerged and drove off in her pink Jaguar. Then there were only the handyman and the maid keeping vigil atop the beautiful knoll, whose curving private driveway discouraged both pedlars and sight-seers with its black-painted wrought-iron gate.

Everything, including the lives of the principal actors, seemed destined to endure forever. The house, the quiet dignity of the lives of its lord and lady, even their obvious great wealth, appeared to be part of an illogical yet definite immortality.

As Inspector Channing had occasion to speculate later, there was a kind of impersonal detachment in all this, a kind of dream-like quality, that lay in layers over the lives of everyone involved.

There did not appear to be any sordidness at all. Certainly no scandal, no hint of dark deeds or evil connections, or even any discernible reason for what ensued based on any of the usual reasons. The doctor and his lady lived exemplary lives. Their serenity was unmarred by debt-collectors, by lovers — as far as Channing knew at the time — by personality clashes, by jealousy or niggardliness.

There was one thing: the Spences had very few close friends. But even this was understandable for each of them was more or less self-sufficient, controlled, calculating not the kind of people who spent themselves or who gave of themselves.

It was indeed the very improbability of two lives being so utterly serene that most puzzled Inspector Channing, whose profession had shown him every facet of exaggerated emotional spending to the point of bankruptcy.

Crimes were *not* committed by people who had everything and who lived on a plane of total serenity, untouched by stress, and usually this variety of person was in turn not susceptible to the violence of others, especially when they were sufficiently islands unto themselves as to avoid personal involvements. In other words, Doctor Spence and his wife, shunning close friendships, were more immune than most people to the strains of human existence.

As far as Bob Channing was initially concerned, the entire affair lacked an air of substance. There was nothing anyone could reach out and touch. No hatred, no jealousy, no avarice, none of the usual reasons behind a crime.

What he met was the cool superiority of Mrs Spence, which was exactly in character for her, the total bewilderment of the maid, which was also in character, and the dumb bafflement of John Harding, the handyman, which was the way he would react towards anything he did not and could not understand.

Bob Channing told his partner on this

assignment that the only applicable rule-of-thumb was the elemental principle that *someone* had been sufficiently motivated to commit murder, and therefore there *had* been hatred; therefore, they would have to seek out this emotion first, and afterwards attach a name and face to it.

The swiftness with which a murder was resolved always depended upon just how soon a suspect or suspects were identified. Otherwise investigators had to start at the bottom, and if this were the case, there was no hope of an early resolvement.

2

A Thorny Dilemma

It was fitting, in Inspector Channing's view, that Carleton Spence had been killed in his handsome, book-lined, oak-panelled study, by a single knife-thrust. It did not disfigure him, and in fact when Maude had looked in shortly before retiring, she'd thought he was sleeping and hadn't disturbed him.

He was slumped in his chair behind the rosewood desk, body totally loose, head down, both hands in his lap. When Channing first saw the corpse he'd thought it looked too theatrical, as though someone, unwilling to let the doctor appear even in police photographs without his dignity, had carefully arranged the body.

He still wasn't convinced this hadn't happened after his preliminary investigation although as time passed the possibility kept assuming less and less importance.

The knife was gone, of course. Channing didn't expect to be *that* lucky, and not until the day after did a Coroner's report indicate that it had been some kind of very sharp, double-edged weapon with a centre fulness, evidently indicating that the blade had been ground from the middle outward towards both edges.

And the thrust had been made with considerable force, as though the killer had been physically powerful or very excited and angry when he made the killing thrust.

Channing had asked if the knife might not have been thrown. The Coroner's man had said he didn't believe it could have been for two reasons. One, there would have been some deviation up or down, and there was neither. Two, in order to penetrate as deeply and with as much force, the knife would have had to have been heavily weighted, which did not seem likely since the hilt had not left a bruise.

The killing had taken place sometime after dinner and before Doctor Spence's bedtime. Mrs Spence said it was common for him to go into his study and pore over his books or bank statements after dinner, but she also said she had heard nothing at all to indicate he hadn't been alone, although obviously *someone* had been closeted with him. And no, she did not interrupt him when he was in the study because his work, whatever it was, property-management or medical research, required solitude for concentration.

There was no collection of weapons, including old daggers, round the house, as Channing had frequently encountered in his line of work. In fact, except for a pearl-handled automatic pistol upstairs in Doctor Spence's bedroom, there wasn't a weapon in the house that Mrs Spence knew of, or that the police search turned up.

Motivation? Mrs Spence could imagine none at all. Her husband paid his bills, did not offend people needlessly, had no indelicate involvements, and although he was probably the object of some dislike, some jealousy, she had never heard him mention a deadly enemy, nor had she ever had reason to think one might exist, although evidently one *did* exist.

Mary Martin and John Harding were just as lacking in illumination for Inspector Channing. There had, to their knowledge, been no attempts at burglary in the years they'd lived at the villa and worked for Doctor Spence. In fact, according to Harding life at the Spence estate was always very quiet, unruffled, totally restful. If it had not been, said Harding, he couldn't have remained because he'd had a series of nervous disorders resulting from prolonged combat activity in Korea; his only therapy was peace and quiet.

Joseph Barthelmess, Channing's associate on the Spence assignment, a blocky, dark-eyed man in his thirties with a sardonic manner, said murder had been committed, without any question, by a poltergeist, because there was no one capable of doing it among Carleton Spence's acquaintances.

Doctor Bill Linden, at the clinic on Sunset Boulevard, was more pragmatic. 'Doctor Spence wasn't altogether lovable except to his patients, and I'm not sure all of them, the men at least, were charmed. Default on a payment meant immediate and swift legal action. Protest against charges resulted in quick transfer to some other hospital. Still, Spence's patients were invariably past the age of violence, Inspector. Even if their physical condition, generally speaking, wasn't incapable of that much exertion, their mental condition was. Doctor Spence's speciality was geriatrics — the care of elderly people.'

Inspector Channing's investigation, instead of becoming less involved as time passed, became more so. He told Inspector Barthelmess to do the routine things one did when medical men were involved with the law. 'Check out his narcotics records, look for a little swindle, a little Last Will and Testament altering, the usual things.'

Co-operation was faultless. If anyone shed any tears over the fatal knifing of Doctor Spence they shed them in private; Channing didn't detect a single red eye, not even the day of the murder — or rather, the morning it was discovered subsequent to the actual slaying. Maude Spence was solemn, reticent, but obviously quite in command, and so was everyone else.

Barthelmess told Channing on the drive back from Spence's magnificent Moorish mansion, it was like being involved in someone else's dream.

No one held back information. They even volunteered it, but it didn't help much, any of it, and Channing's remark to Barthelmess was that what they needed wasn't so much help, what they needed was one disgruntled, one significant, cold word of accusation.

Furthermore, Spence's narcotics records were in perfect order. He had accounted for every gram used, and what remained locked up at the clinic balanced out exactly with the amount of the stuff supposed to be there. But as Doctor Linden said, 'You're barking up the wrong tree, Inspector Channing. The most a physician can make from peddling narcotics is something like twenty-five thousand dollars a year.'

'It's a very respectable sum, Doctor.'

'Not to a man like Doctor Spence, Inspector, whose annual income is well up into the six-figure bracket. What sense would it make for him to take the risk?'

'But they do it, Doctor, right along.'

Linden shook his head. 'Not men like Carleton Spence. Never men like that.'

Bill Linden was right of course. The more Channing dug into Carleton Spence's background the more convinced he became Linden was right. The man who emerged under Channing's pitiless digging was close, cold, egotistical, completely self-immersed and calculatingly practical. He wouldn't grab at a chance to make twenty-five thousand dollars, instead he would stand back a moment and consider what would be involved. Then, and only then, he would reach forth providing there was no risk. He had long since passed the stage in life where he had to take risks. By Channing's estimate, arrived at through a good deal of digging and totalling up, Carleton Spence at the time of his murder was worth very close to three million dollars.

Joe Barthelmess liked that figure. 'There's your reason. How many murders have you been assigned to where someone was killed for a tenth that much money.'

'Who?' asked Channing. 'The widow?' He began wagging his head before Barthelmess could answer. 'I'd like her too, but for a couple of things. One of them is that a man plunged that knife into her husband, not a woman. The other thing is — why? She'd have inherited from him anyway, and according to the servants, who would certainly know, they were happily married. So — who killed him for the money or his property?'

Barthelmess was dogged. 'The widow, and I don't care *how* she got him knifed, I only know from talking to Doctor Spence's attorney yesterday, that she inherits the house and the bank accounts.'

'Who gets all the rentals and commercial properties, not to mention that clinic that pays off like a broken slot-machine?'

'Janie Ford.'

Channing hadn't known that. He'd

met Janie and her father, Frank Ford, the stooped, scholarly-looking widowed father of Janie. He looked steadily at Barthelmess. 'And you think the widow is it?'

Barthelmess nodded, still dogged. 'Sure. As for Janie, she's out of it if the widow sues to break the Will.'

'Whose opinion is that?'

'Spence's attorney. I had a long talk with him yesterday.'

'Did he happen to tell you how it was that Spence, a phony old iceberg happened to get involved with a sweet young thing like Janie Ford, every man's ideal of the Young American Girl?'

'You're pretty sarcastic for so early in the morning,' said Barthelmess before answering the question. 'Yeah, the attorney said Spence told him Janie was his idea of what his daughter would have been like if he'd ever had a daughter.'

Channing was very sceptical. 'Likely. Did you happen to see Janie the day I spoke to her father?'

'I saw her, and I'll admit she didn't put *me* in mind of the daughter I never had.

Not in that cream-coloured cardigan and those beige slacks.'

'Then maybe we've got something after all,' said Channing, beginning to brighten a little. 'A secret connection. An affair between Miss All-American Girl and a rich man who fooled everyone into thinking all he cared about was his big ego and his bank accounts and his real estate.'

Barthelmess adopted a distressed expression. 'Bob, he'd have told her he was leaving her a fortune in property; why would she kill him over that, when by *not* killing she'd get it all eventually anyway, and without any risk at all.'

'I didn't say *she* killed him,' said Channing, thinking of the Coroner's report on the power behind the arm that guided the murder weapon. 'I simply implied she might be worth investigating. Maybe she had a jealous lover in the background. Look Joe, we've got to start *somewhere*.' Channing made a strained smile. 'There's no butler.'

'Bum joke,' said Barthelmess, not keen about going through all the labour involved in investigating Janie Ford when it seemed so improbable anything would come of it. 'What about Carter Spence; of them all, he fits the description of a guy who not only didn't care much for the doctor, but who had the power to skewer him.'

'I'm checking him out,' said Channing. 'He wired that he'd be arriving here within the next few days from British Columbia, which you'll have to concede is one hell of a long way to reach, to stick a knife into someone down here.'

'How about Doctor Linden at the clinic?'

'He could have driven in the knife, but what's the motivation? Janie inherits the clinic, he doesn't. Spence paid him damned well, by his own admission, and now that's all in jeopardy.'

Barthelmess said, in exasperation, 'Are you trying to find the murderer or find reasons not to find him? It had to be a man. There are Ford, the nephew, Harding the servant, Doctor Linden, that we know of. Another three or four others will probably turn up before we button it all up.'

'But you still like Mrs Spence for the role.'

'Dammit, Bob, I said I liked her as the *reason* someone used that pig-sticker on the doctor. And believe me she's cold enough for something like murder not to phase her at all. Did she cry or moan or fling herself down or faint? Hell no; she stood there like something carved from marble.'

'Joe, I just can't see a female of her type reacting any other way — to murder or anything else. She's like you just said, carved from marble. But unless we can turn up something in her background, which I doubt at this moment, she's simply going to turn out to be just what she looks and act like, a cold-blooded woman.'

'How about Janie; would you call her cold-blooded?'

Channing smiled slightly. 'Hardly. She's alive in every square inch of hide. She tingles to every nerve-end. It seemed so incongruous that she'd be a psychology

Major at the University I telephoned to a friend of mine over there.'

'And what did he say?'

'You wouldn't believe it.'

'Try me.'

'He said vibrant Janie is as dull, as quiet, as unapproachable as any pretty girl he's ever seen. That she studies hard, gets high marks, and always wears loose clothing so her figure won't show up and give anyone ideas.'

Barthelmess inclined his head. 'You're right, I wouldn't believe it.'

3

No Suspects

For Inspector Channing the Spence
murder case was one of those crimes
that did not involve a policeman in any
kind of personal concern. Doctor Spence
kept coming through as a man Channing
didn't particularly care for but whom he
didn't actually dislike. And the physical
act of murder hadn't been especially gory,
so he felt no revulsion for the unidentified
murderer. In short, he could approach
the crime from a nice, clean, academic
viewpoint, which is precisely how he did
approach it.

But just as academically, it kept eluding
him. He couldn't put forth a hand and
touch anything. There was a dead
man — unlovable — and a murderer,
unknown, whose crime had been almost
clinically perfect.

When Carter Spence arrived four

days after his uncle's passing Inspector Channing at last found someone he could talk frankly to. Not *entirely* frankly because in Channing's line of work one learned very early on, that keeping things to oneself was very often profitable. Still, he and Carter Spence and Joe Barthelmess went to lunch together, and there, although they only met a half hour earlier, Channing found Carter Spence earthy, uncomplicated, blunt and believable.

'I don't know enough to help,' said Spence, eating a great, rare steak in the middle of the day that awed Barthelemess. 'As I said back in the office, my uncle was a seven-dollar bill as far as I was concerned. I told him he was a phony when he wanted me to manage his property for him. As for this new wife, I've never even seen a picture of her. Until you wired I had no idea he'd got himself a wife. As for whom I'd suspect — it's more of a waste of time for me to answer you, Inspector, than it would be for you to listen, because I don't know his friends or associates. And except

27

for me, he has no blood-relatives.'

'Motive?' said Channing, half smiling.

Carter Spence didn't smile back. He wasn't the subtle type. 'Give me your pen and I'll write it on this napkin, Inspector. I'll forego anything from his estate including cash and property. Does that sound as if I'd have motivation?'

Barthelmess was instantly suspicious. 'You wouldn't accept anything he left you?'

'Not a stinking dime.'

'Mind explaining?'

'Look, Inspector, I make sixty-five thousand a year. I own property in my own right. I'm damned independent by nature and I can stand almost any kind of man but the kind of phony he was. I don't need his gratuity and wouldn't accept it.'

'I don't think you'll have to,' said Channing quietly. 'It all goes to his widow and to the daughter of the man who manages his income property. His name is Frank Ford, the girl's name is Janie Ford.'

Spence looked surprised. 'A girl? You

mean a *young* girl?'

'Twenty-one or two. Very pretty. A psychology Major at the University.'

'Why that dirty old devil,' said candid Carter Spence. 'And him just married.'

Channing smiled. 'I didn't say Doctor Spence had anything going with this girl. I only said . . . '

'Oh hell,' growled Carter Spence with loud and lingering scorn. 'Who are you trying to kid, if not yourself, Inspector? You should have known that old fake.'

Channing didn't pursue this subject. He'd had the same initial reaction. Not only that, but he still felt convinced Carter Spence wasn't exactly right. But all things in good time; if there *had* been some kind of unpleasant connection it would come out, and right now he wasn't too concerned on that score anyway. What he needed was a brawny arm, or at least one that could, under sufficient stimulus, become powerfully enough motivated.

Carter Spence had such an arm. In fact, he was built like a football player, or like a man who had used his body hard all his life, knew no other way to use it, and had been in brawls from Singapore to St Louis — which wasn't too far from the facts at that. Ten years in the army, as a sergeant for the last seven of those years, didn't soften a man up much.

'In the past,' he said, sipping coffee after finishing his meal, 'you might have heard uncomplimentary things said about your uncle, Mister Spence. Joe and I are in the position of the proverbial drowning man We're eager for any kind of straw.'

Carter Spence grimaced. 'I remember my father saying once that even as a kid his brother had been the biggest fake and most conceited kid in his class. But you'll play hell involving my father. He's been dead twelve years. Boys, I just never sought out my uncle. I hadn't seen him in ten years until he asked me to come and see him. I don't know anyone he knows.'

'But you came when I wired you he'd been murdered,' said Channing.

'You *asked* me to come, Inspector. Otherwise I'd have been perfectly content to read about it in the newspapers. The guy means nothing to me. Less, as a matter of fact, than any of the labour crews I boss up in Canada.'

'Then you disliked him,' said Barthelmess, and got a witheringly direct and truculent look.

'I've been trying to get it across to you guys,' growled the big man, 'that I dislike his *type*. I always have. They're the con men, the smooth operators, the barracks lawyers, the phonies and fakes who do their damnedest to live off everyone else. Him, as a person, I didn't give a damn for one way or another. He was exactly what I told him he was — a phony. But it wasn't *personal*. It couldn't have been. I didn't have to look at him nor listen to him. He just belonged to a *type* I've never cared for. That answer you, Barthelmess?'

It did, and Joe nodded. It also amused him, being hit over the head with words. Usually, when he talked to people, particularly if they were involved in some serious felony, they were very careful. Not this ham-handed man from British Columbia who had eyes like wet agates and a forthright power to him that didn't leave people in much doubt about his opinion of them for very long.

'But he's dead,' said Barthelmess. 'Someone rammed half a yard of steel through his chest.'

'So find the guy who did it,' said Spence with characteristic roughness. '*I* didn't. Even if I'd wanted to it'd have been pretty damned hard, being in British Columbia the hour he was killed.'

On the stroll back to police headquarters where Spence had left his car, Channing wondered aloud why no one had encountered the killer when he entered the house. Of course he and Barthelmess had heard the handyman's story; he hadn't heard a car drive in and hadn't been round front where he'd have seen one in any case, but then he just didn't think anyone had driven in, because it was so quiet around the estate, from his room off the end of the garage, he ordinarily heard every sound.

And Mary Martin, who usually opened the door to callers, hadn't been summoned all that evening. In fact, she hadn't been summoned all that afternoon and evening.

Spence said, 'The guy came on foot. He hid his car down the road somewhere and slipped in on foot. He'd hardly drive right up if he had a bayonet or something under his coat to kill someone with, would he?'

Channing mildly agreed. 'Arriving doesn't really worry me too much, Mister Spence; it's getting inside the house that's got me wondering.'

'My uncle let the guy in. How else?'

'Seems likely,' said Channing, still mild, still agreeable. So mild in fact Carter Spence threw him a long, critical look, as though he were wondering how such a man had ever achieved the position Channing held.

Then Spence shrugged. 'It looks to me like about all that is required is a little backtracking. Someone was coming to see my uncle that night after supper. Someone he expected and met at the door.'

'Why didn't this someone ring the bell like everyone else does when they arrive at a house, expected or not?'

'How do you know he *didn't* ring it?'

'It wasn't rung. The maid didn't hear and neither did anyone else. It wasn't rung.'

That stopped Spence for a moment, until he said quietly, 'Well, the guy knocked instead of using the bell.' When neither Barthelmess or Channing commented on that, Spence shrugged again. 'Damned if I know.'

Channing finally looked up, smiling. 'That's the point,' he told the other man. 'And every other avenue opens up about the same way. Damned if I know.'

They parted out front of the police station with Carter Spence saying he'd drive out and meet his aunt-in-law or whatever she was, and offer his help, although he had no idea what he could do even if she took him up on the offer — which neither Channing nor Barthelmess expected her to do — and afterwards he'd check back with Channing in a day or two, and if there was no further need for him to hang about, he'd head back for British Columbia.

It was exactly the kind of attitude and statement Channing expected from Carter Spence. He watched the big, burly man stride away with a light spring to his step, then turned and followed Barthelmess on inside.

Joe was calm, probably because there were no longer any wrinkles in his stomach, as they sat down to go over things again in Channing's cubby-hole office. Joe was also impressed with Carter Spence.

'The guy's larger than life,' he said. 'Big, strong as an ox, and as simple as day and night.' He caught Channing's eyes on him and quickly added: 'But I'll run a check on him anyway, routine stuff with the Department of Defence, stuff like that.'

Channing nodded, then mentioned something that indicated he hadn't been as sceptical of Carter Spence as he'd looked. 'Why does pretty Janie act two parts, one at home around her father, the other at the University where she's an honour-bright student?'

Barthelmess took the short-cut to arrive at what he thought might be behind Channing's remark. 'She was living two lives. One at school, one around her father and Doctor Spence. So they had something going on the sly, old Spence and Miss Peaches-And-Cream. It's not exactly the most original story under the sun, Bob.'

Channing didn't look elated but he said, 'Maybe. At least we've got to start *somewhere*. You take Linden at the clinic and work back to Mrs Spence and the servants. I'll go over to the University, then work back through Janie's friends, maybe as far as her father.'

'That'll shoot the day.'

'All right. We'll meet here in the morning and put our little pointed heads together to either clear Janie or turn up something nasty enough to lead us to something else.'

It was, as Channing had said, a start, and although it did not appear as a very promising one, at least it was something, for otherwise there was little enough.

For Inspector Channing the drive to the University was less nostalgic than it might have been, his mind being otherwise occupied, but he had grown up in the community immediately northeastward from Santa Monica, and had himself graduated from the University of California at Los Angeles, commonly called U.C.L.A., or just plain UCLA, which was his destination now.

But when Channing had graduated there had been a definite line of demarcation between Westwood Village where the University was, and Santa Monica, which lay upon the shore of the Pacific Ocean. Now, there was no such demarcation; the two places blended and scarcely anyone referred to Westwood as a 'village' any more. It was a town of hundreds of thousands of people. UCLA, once its primary source of revenue, was now just an enormous sprawl of academic red brick.

And Channing wasn't all that old. The growth of Southern California had been so incredible for the preceding quarter century that two-thirds of its current residents had only been in the State that long.

As for the University, what had once been a handsome, clean establishment bounded by scenic Sunset Boulevard on one side, Westwood Village on the other side, was now a series of tumbled red-brick blocks scattered over a campus that had shrunk until it was little more than a city within a city.

Channing found a parking place, sighed over the fact that he would have to walk nearly a mile to reach his destination — the Criminology Building — and set forth through as beautiful a springtime day as he'd ever seen, which took some of the complaint out of his thoughts, and on the way he passed some of the most attractive female students he'd ever seen, too, and that winnowed out the last of his mild discontent.

4

Routine Processes

Gerald Wheaton was a retired detective from the Los Angeles Police Department, although he scarcely seemed old enough, and when Inspector Channing finally reached him, Wheaton was sitting in a tiny room with a hazy view of grass and trees and the shrunken campus gardens, feet propped on the sill, smoking his pipe.

He was pleased to see his visitor, even offered to brew some coffee at the electric hot-plate and percolator nearby. Channing declined but drew up a chair and sat facing the window to also enjoy the view, or bemoan the lack of it. He said, 'About that girl I telephoned you for information on, Gerry . . . '

'I guessed that when I saw you come through the door,' replied Wheaton. 'It's not very often I get real ones to be interested in, nowadays, Bob. I ran a little check on her.'

'How did she come out?'

'Not too odd,' said Wheaton, and puffed a moment before speaking again. 'She had a relatively recent change of address. From Hollywood she moved to Santa Monica, but you'd have picked that up by now.'

Channing hadn't done any such thing but refrained from saying so.

'Her father's a book-keeper, accountant, good head with figures, and at one time he taught right here at UCLA Economics Department. The girl came directly to the University from Santa Monica High School.'

'I thought you said they lived in Hollywood.'

Wheaton puffed and nodded. 'They did. Before Hollywood they lived in Santa Monica. The father goes where he gets work.'

'I see. Go on.'

'The girl doesn't date on campus. Doesn't do anything to draw attention to herself. Asked Moe Delaney in her psychology unit about her. He said she's normal enough, that it's fairly common for studious girls — and boys — to keep social and academic lives separate.'

'Doesn't sound very normal to me, Gerry,' said Channing, and the criminologist laughed.

'When you were here, Bob, you wouldn't have noticed this kind of girl at all.'

Channing conceded. 'Probably not. Gerry, as I mentioned over the telephone earlier, this doctor who was killed left the girl better than a million dollars worth of choice income property, and yet there was nothing to link them together at all, beyond the fact that her father was the manager of property for Doctor Spence.'

'How does the father strike you?' asked Wheaton. 'I mean — here's a guy who's barely scraped along all these years suddenly managing choice, lucrative rentals . . . If he was worrying over the girl's future, he might view his current position as very probably the best opportunity so far to do something about it.'

'Like murder?'

'Why not?'

Channing didn't know why not. He'd spoken to Janie's father, hadn't been very impressed with anything about the man, neither his appearance which was nondescript, his strength, which seemed conspicuous because of its probable absence, nor Frank Ford's personality, which had seemed as colourless as possible.

Channing said, 'The man's certainly anything but an ideal suspect.'

Wheaton, the lifetime cop, said cynically, 'What the hell is an ideal suspect, Bob?'

Channing smiled, let it pass, and said, 'I'll look into that angle,' but apart from the physical obstacles, such as how a man with as little force and subtlety as Ford possessed could ever talk as strong, as seasoned and devious a person as Carleton Spence into changing his Will, there was the lack of any worthwhile relationship between Ford and Spence. Even granting there might have been some clandestine affair between the doctor and the girl, it still didn't seem that Spence would be that carried away. It was out of character for him. At least on that basis.

Wheaton interrupted Channing's reveries with a question. 'What about the widow?'

'Like Churchill once said — a mystery within an enigma.'

'You've checked her out?'

'Still working on it, Gerry, but except for an early and unworkable marriage, and a man-hating existence for the next fifteen years, she's clean.'

'Evidently she got over being a man-hater,' said Wheaton dryly. 'Three million dollars worth.'

Channing nodded. 'At forty they need social security. Anyway, she's one of those self-contained individuals — predictable, unimaginative, cold. Doesn't seem to have a tear-duct in her anywhere. If I were picking someone for the role of plotter, she'd head the list.'

'But you're not?'

'Coroner says a *man* had to push that knife into the doctor.'

'She had a friend?'

'I'm working on that angle.'

'But somehow you like the girl for complicity. Well; it's possible, except for what Moe Delaney in Psychology says, she's not capable of gory violence. She'd break down, go into hysterics, something like that.'

'How about the psychological angle?'

'Such as?'

'Well, she's been studying behaviour, patterns of conduct, personality formats, stuff like that.'

'If you mean, would she know how to get some man to kill Doctor Spence, the answer would be — probably. But what stumps me, and what you've got to thresh out first, is how in hell she got Spence to put her in his Will.' Wheaton removed the pipe and set it aside. He couldn't talk and keep the pipe going at the same time, which was probably why so many pipe-smokers became taciturn. 'If, as you say, Spence wasn't emotional enough to be influenced by some torrid love affair, then I think that'll be your key to — something. If not the actual crime, then to something that will reveal *how* the crime came to be committed. The girl will very likely be your key, Bob.'

After a little more casual conversation, Channing went back out into the spring-time sunshine, hotter now but still quite pleasant, thanks to an off-shore breeze coming over the sea to the nearby land.

He had thought he might use up the rest of the afternoon seeking friends of Janie Ford, but when he reached his car he gave that idea up for several reasons, the most obvious one being that anyone he talked to would probably telephone Janie and expose him, and decided to go directly to see her father. It might amount to the same thing, but aside from the fact that sooner or later Janie was going to realize she was involved, there was the possibility that her father, who would know he'd be on the list of people the police were interested in, would treat a visit from Channing as one of the inevitable police routines.

Ford did, as a matter of fact, treat it like that. He was pleasant if a little distant, when Channing reached his residence, on Sixteenth Street in Santa Monica, which stood slightly higher than the central district and was therefore more susceptible to the sea breezes.

It was a cottage, old but well kept, and out at the back where Ford took Channing, there was a delightful little garden showing ample evidence of thoughtful care. The grass was close-cropped, emerald green, and the borders of roses, zinnias, other vivid colours and sizes of annuals and perennials, blazed forth in response to care and affection.

Frank Ford himself, stooped, scholarly, grey and somehow withdrawn in a gentle, quiet way, was not a man Channing would have glanced twice at in a crowd, nor cultivated socially. He was colourless. Even when the talk got round to Janie, he seemed, if not actually indifferent, then certainly impersonal. His wife, he said, had died when Janie had been twelve years old. Since then he had been both mother and father. He was a native of the Los Angeles area, which was unusual but not unheard of, and had been engaged in his current profession all his mature life.

Channing encouraged the man to talk

about himself. They had talked before, but very briefly, the day after the murder, and now, listening to Frank Ford, Channing got the impression the man was totally indifferent to the murder.

He thought that would be quite in character for a man who seemed to actually have little more than a monk's personal feelings about things outside his own little world.

Then Ford made a remark that brought Channing's interest up at once. He mentioned knowing Doctor Spence prior to taking the job as manager for Spence.

'It was a good many years ago; he was practising medicine in Hollywood at that time. I had just opened an office on Ventura Boulevard. I didn't actually do any of his work, then, but I showed him how to set up a simple set of books.' Ford looked at Channing with no lustre in his eyes. 'He was a very handsome man in those days.' Ford looked back at his garden. 'That was about it — until we met again when he was looking for someone to manage his properties.'

'You didn't see him in the interim?'

Ford shook his head, still looking at the garden. 'No reason,' he said. 'After my wife died I hardly thought about the man at all.' A little smile flickered over Ford's pale features. 'It's a full time occupation, being father and mother, counsellor and baby-sitter, Inspector Channing.'

'I'm sure it is,' murmured the detective. 'As you know, Doctor Spence left the real estate to Janie . . .'

Ford shook his head. 'I didn't know,' he said, without looking excited, elated, displeased, nor even surprised.

Channing pressed on. 'There would be a good reason, Mister Ford. I'm trying to figure it out.'

'In relation to his murder, Inspector? Believe me, Janie isn't involved. You don't know her but I do.'

Channing pondered: How did you ask a father if his daughter were having an affair with an older man? You didn't. Channing said, 'But the doctor was murdered.'

'Not by Janie. That's utterly ridiculous.'

'I'd like to be convinced of that, Mister Ford. You are an experienced enough person to realize that there is bound to be curiosity over Spence leaving Janie over a million dollars worth of very lucrative — and valuable — income property.'

Ford turned and studied Channing. 'And so you think she killed him?'

'No. I'm simply trying to work out the relationship.'

Ford kept staring. His neck reddened, then his face. 'I see. You suspect a liaison. An illicit affair.'

'No again, Mister Ford. You're anticipating me.'

'I have a protective instinct, Inspector.'

'Of course,' retorted Channing, with forbearance. 'I understand. But *you've* got to understand something. I'll go blundering into a lot of places that have little to do with the actual crime before I get wherever I'm going in this mess. I'm not accusing your daughter of anything illicit, nor even illegal. I'm simply trying to find out why Spence would make her part of his Will.'

Ford, perhaps soothed a little by Channing's calmness, looked away. 'He had no children you know. He was a complex man, but when I came to work for him managing the properties, he took an interest in Janie. *Paternal* interest, Inspector. He grew quite fond of her.' Ford shrugged. 'I suppose that's why he left her the property. There surely could be no other reason.'

Channing had to be content with that, at least for the time being, and as he left the house, Frank Ford strolling to the car at the kerbing with him, Channing had the feeling that getting through Ford's habitual detachment wouldn't be easy.

The man said, 'Inspector, if Mrs Spence wishes, I'm sure she can contest Doctor Spence's Will. I've seen it done before.'

This wasn't part of Channing's concern except insofar as it might impinge upon what definitely *was* his concern. He passed it off by saying, 'I suppose she can, Mister Ford.'

They stood beside the car a moment gazing at one another. Whatever Ford's thoughts, Channing's were relatively direct. He hadn't been helped much by this visit nor this man, and Ford gave the impression that even if he had known anything, he wouldn't have been very co-operative. Not out of malice, particularly, but simply out of detachment.

On the drive back to his office Channing labelled Ford a strange one. The man didn't seem very excited over having his daughter become rich, practically overnight. But on the credit side, it didn't strike Channing as probable that even the Second Coming would upset Ford very much.

A strange one indeed.

5

Some Queries

Joe Barthelmess reported the next morning that he'd spent an interesting afternoon with Doctor Linden at Spence's private clinic, and never got round to visiting Mrs Spence, as he'd hoped to do.

Bill Linden, Joe told Channing, was a realist. Inspector Channing was interested in a definition of that term. 'He sees things as black and white,' explained Barthelmess. 'For example, he said Spence was a competent enough physician and a fair surgeon, but that he was mediocre, not as outstanding as he believed himself to be, and as he somehow always managed to convince his patients he was. Linden's not bitter; his point is simply that Spence was a money-grabber rather than a topnotch practitioner.'

Channing wasn't impressed. 'I think

the doctor's personality has come through clearly enough,' he said. 'What else did Linden have to say that was pertinent to his demise?'

'Nothing at all, and he levelled with me right down the line. He doesn't know anything, Bob.' Suddenly Barthelmess screwed up his face. 'But there was one thing: When we finished hiking up and down the corridors while he read charts and gave instructions to his nurses, we went to his office. The connecting door led into Doctor Spence's office. Linden explained about the door, then he said, 'Mrs Spence spent most of yesterday afternoon in there,' meaning in Spence's private office.'

'You had a look in?'

'Yes. Files, desk drawers, appointment calendars, nothing unusual that I saw, but that's the point in mentioning Mrs Spence. Granting she had the right — what could she have removed?'

'Good point,' murmured Channing, and glanced at his wrist. 'I'm on my way out there. I'll see if she cares to consider me as a confidant.'

Barthelmess made a snorting sound. 'That'll be the day. That woman's as likely to make a cop her confidant as I am to fly to the moon.'

'You want to be careful about saying things like that, Joe. They're no longer valid. I can visualize you on the moon no later than year after next.'

But of course Barthelmess was correct. The very beautiful widow received Channing into a cool, deathly silent house that smelt of flowers, ushered him to a sitting room and although she was dressed for going out — shopping possibly — she sat with a boundless patience while he asked his questions.

She knew, she said, after talking to her husband's attorney, how the estate had been divided, and it didn't show in her eyes or in her expression that she was the least bit resentful. She even said approximately the same thing Frank Ford had said.

'Doctor Spence had no children of his own. He was fond of them.'

Channing nodded, thinking that lovely Janie in that cardigan and those beige slacks was hardly a child. He said, 'It's been a week now, Mrs Spence, you surely have come to some conclusions. Would you share them with me?'

She would not, but she declined saying that in so many words, instead, she smiled faintly and made a little fluttery gesture with her hands. 'I'm more at a loss than you are, Inspector. My husband had no enemies that I knew of. He had his work, his investments . . . ' She shrugged as though incapable of believing a man could need anything more. 'As for the girl: A nice little thing. I did once discuss her with Carleton. He said he was considering using her as receptionist at the clinic when she finished school. That was all.'

Channing was left with the awkward question of an affair. He fidgeted slightly and gazed round the lovely room. Mrs Spence picked his brains, which wasn't much of an accomplishment, since she was a worldly woman and Janie was very attractive.

She said, 'I think not, Inspector.'

Channing brought his gaze back. She

was watching him with that serene, utterly calm look he'd encountered on her face the morning of the removal of her husband's body. Another strange one, he thought, then she spoke on.

'Of course it has occured to me that you'd wonder about an affair between the girl and my husband. I only knew the girl casually, but I knew Doctor Spence very well. Even if he'd been inclined, I can assure you that I knew his schedule so well I'd have suspected at once if he'd made any departure from it.'

And she would, too, Channing believed. He said, 'How long would it, take for them to meet, Mrs Spence; an hour, two hours?' It was a cynical thing to say but it had merit.

She remained adamant. 'I'd have known, Inspector, believe me.'

He had to be content with that, so he struck out in a new direction. 'I understand you can contest the Will.'

'Yes,' she replied, meaning that topic had come up in her discussion with the attorney. 'But I have no intention of doing so at this time.'

'That's very generous of you, Mrs Spence.'

The beautiful face showed nothing. 'It was his money, his property, Inspector. Moreover, I'm very wealthy as a result of my share.'

There was no denying that. The problem was simply that Channing couldn't get through the serene woman's facade to find out if she were sincere in saying it or not. Not many people, with even less excuse than she had for breaking a Will and acquiring even more riches, would not do so.

'There's the estate tax,' he murmured. 'Inheritances seem to be something Uncle Sam pounces on with both hands.'

'There will still be a great deal left.'

She sat watching him, unruffled, very handsome, perfectly groomed and calculatingly icy. He felt like sighing. Instead he said, 'You were married before, Mrs Spence?'

That was the only time during their entire visit he detected a shadow in her glance. And even then it came and went very swiftly, a faint, swift passing of dark and unpleasant recollection. She nodded. 'When I was much younger, Inspector. But if you know I was married you've undoubtedly dug into that. You won't need anything from me about it.'

'I didn't dig, Mrs Spence, so I'd like your version.'

She moved, crossed one leg over the other, looked at the hands lying in her lap, then softly spoke. 'It has no bearing at all upon my relationship with Doctor Spence.'

Channing didn't speak. He sat looking at her and waiting. She saw that he wasn't going to back off, so she spoke again, softly and incisively.

'I was young, Inspector, he was handsome. It was one of those biological things. It lasted slightly more than a year, then he left and when I heard from him in Reno, I didn't contest the divorce. I haven't seen him to this day.'

She raised her lovely eyes and at last they were human, with pain and something else — hatred? — in their liquid depths. Channing was satisfied. He would probably check it out, but

58

not mandatorily; not unless it featured in whatever came next. He said, 'No children, Mrs Spence?'

She shook her head avoiding his glance, then she rose. 'Unless there is something else, I have an appointment in the city.'

The 'city' meant Los Angeles; no one living in Santa Monica referred to it as a city. He rose too. 'I'd like to look at the study again, if I might.'

She took him to the doorway and as he passed by there was a delicate fragrance of some very expensive perfume around her. She turned as the maid appeared. Mary Martin's alert but unintentional eyes jumped from one face to the other with a lively interest. She said, 'Ma'am, John got your car out.' It seemed to be a reminder that Mrs Spence had to leave.

Channing waited until the maid had departed before saying it wouldn't be necessary for Mrs Spence to wait on his account; he could let himself out when he was finished.

She nodded but hung there a moment looking into his face as though she had a question in mind. He smiled. 'Just a look around that's all. You see, until I figure out how the killer got in here without anyone but Doctor Spence knowing he'd arrived, I'm in a quandry.'

She nodded softly. 'I'm sorry that I can't help. But he did, occasionally, receive people at the door and take them to the study while I was upstairs or in the garden.'

'Didn't they ring the bell?'

She debated that a moment. 'If I was in the garden I wouldn't have heard it.'

'But Mary Martin would have.'

Again she debated. 'It's not mandatory, Inspector. Mary's quarters are off the rear pantry. If she were in her room she might not have heard.'

He had to settle for that although it occurred to him that after dinner Mary Martin would probably be cleaning up in the kitchen. He nodded and smiled. 'Thank you.' He watched her cross the hall, cross part of the yonder room where they'd been sitting, then disappear. She was a beautiful creature, front or rear.

He sighed, turned and gazed round the elegant, masculine study. He'd gone over it before. The windows, for instance, which were leaded and opened off the front of the house, were locked from the inside. That's the way they'd been when he'd first arrived on the scene while Doctor Spence was hanging dead in his desk-chair.

Of course, if the murderer had been *inside* the house there'd have been no need to lock them, assuming they weren't locked before the killing, but he'd ascertained from the light film of dust on his first visit, that they hadn't been opened, which didn't prove anything, but it substantiated what he'd already deduced — that the murderer had been taken into the study by Doctor Spence, and hadn't climbed through any windows.

As for departure, that would have been even easier, for unless someone had inadvertently come upon the man leaving, there was no need for him to be exposed; the route from the study door, which opened off the hall, was directly to the front door, a distance of some fifteen or twenty feet. After that, out into the darkness and away.

The study offered no encouragement. In fact, the first time Channing had visited it, the fact that the killer had faced his victim, indicating they knew one another, had precluded the theory that perhaps the murderer had been waiting, in hiding, for his victim.

There were no hiding places in any case. The walls, book-lined for the most part, offered no such avenues. There was only the one door leading into the room, so the killer couldn't have slipped in some other way.

Channing was convinced that the room, beyond being dumb witness to murder, held no keys to the solution of the crime at all. He did as he'd said he'd do, made a cursory little examination, then departed.

It was when he was leaving that he noticed how easy it was to pass from the study to the front door and outside, without making any noise and also without being visible, except for the first five feet, to anyone who might be sitting in the living-room across the hallway.

It also occurred to him that the murderer would more than likely have verified this fact in advance of his final — and fatal — visit.

On the drive back to headquarters he stopped off at a small restaurant, noisy with the bustle of noontime, had a light lunch of salad and tea, and decided to get Mary Martin, and Maude Spence too, if necessary, to provide him with a list of everyone who had called recently — everyone, in other words, who would want to know how easy it was to reach the study and to afterwards reach the front door again.

This thought prompted another: how would the killer, after ascertaining that he could get in and out again with minimal risk, devise a plan to make certain Doctor Spence would be in the study the night he was to murder his victim?

That had a simple answer: Since the man knew the doctor, he could call, make an appointment, and arrive just late enough so that Doctor Spence would begin to wonder; would possibly be waiting in the study.

Of course, if Doctor Spence had *not* been waiting, had *not* been on hand to admit the killer without anyone else knowing it, then the murderer simply would not have killed Spence that night. He'd have waited for another, better, opportunity. Which meant of course he would have come in and visited. And *that* meant the murderer of Doctor Spence was known to everyone in the house.

A stranger would hardly know as much as the killer knew, certainly not about the house, the habits of the victim, the opportune time to kill Spence. But then a stranger would hardly have killed Doctor Spence anyway.

As he completed his drive back, Channing smiled a little. He had *something*, finally. Not very much, but more than he'd had before driving to the Spence estate.

6

Janie

One thought nagged at Channing. Throughout his interview with Mrs Spence she hadn't mentioned that her late husband's nephew had been to see her.

It hadn't been necessary for her to do this, of course, and Channing hadn't asked, so plausibly at least, there was no reason to wonder. Still, Channing *did* wonder.

When Joe Barthelmess came in an hour after lunch-time with some facts about the people involved which he'd dug up through various police sources, Channing asked if Carter Spence had called. Barthelmess shook his head, passed it off as unimportant, then handed Channing some notes he'd made.

'John Harding, the handyman at the Spence place, may suffer from bad nerves, but he didn't get it all in Korea. He served five-to-ten for grand larceny after his stint in the army.' Then, as though to minimize this interesting fact, Barthelmess added: 'But he's been clean ever since, and had no previous record.'

Channing studied that particular notation, then put it aside to read the second one. Maude Spence's first husband, the one she'd told Channing she hadn't seen since the day he deserted her to go to Reno and file for divorce, was right here in Los Angeles, owner of a popular bistro. If she hadn't seen him it was difficult for Channing to believe she didn't know where he was. After all, Los Angeles, large as it was, didn't have all that many truly notorious nightspots.

The next note didn't tell Inspector Channing very much; only that Frank Ford's wife had died of an overdose of sleeping pills. Channing held that note longest.

Barthelmess, seeing which note it was, said, 'Suicide. There's an old report on it. But you know how those things are; apart from stating the facts — time, place, cause of death — there is nothing else. No mention of any probable reason.'

No wonder Frank Ford was a brooding, withdrawn man. 'What a hell of a thing to have on your conscience,' said Channing, and carefully put that note aside. 'Anything else?'

'I'm still waiting for the scoop on the nephew. Takes longer clearing that stuff through Army channels. Otherwise — nothing. Linden's almost drab. He's never been anywhere or done anything. College to medical school, medical school to internship, internship to L.A. General, then out to Spence's clinic. No wonder the guy's got that black-and-white outlook.'

Channing mentioned his deductions on the drive to headquarters and Joe Barthelmess wasn't very impressed. 'We already know who *could* have murdered the doctor, and it had to be someone he knew very well, and that everyone else knew him too. But that doesn't narrow the field, Bob. What about Ford?'

Channing didn't have much to say about Ford but he did mention his intention of driving out later in the day and seeing Janie. Barthelmess brushed that aside, he did not consider Janie as important as the person he asked about next.

'What came of the visit to Mrs Spence? She embraced you at the door and immediately took you into her confidence.'

'She did neither. As you said — that'd be the day.'

'I still like her for the part of the wicked witch,' said Barthelmess.

Channing wasn't listening. 'Remember Carter Spence saying he was going out there? Well, I wonder if he did. She didn't mention it.'

Barthelmess pondered. 'Maybe he didn't. Frankly, I don't visualize him as being involved. But when the scoop comes back from army sources we'll know better about that possibility.'

An unexpected visitor arrived while they were recapitulating. Janie Ford walked in looking uncertain about having the correct office or not. Barthelmess rose at once to hold the door wide for her to enter. Channing rose smiling and got a chair. She seemed a little relieved but not entirely so. With two interested detectives gazing at her, she blushed, then said. 'I had it in mind to stop in several days ago, but your building isn't exactly the kind of place one is irresistibly drawn to.'

Joe smiled. 'Would you like some coffee?'

'No thank you.'

'A coke?' Barthelmess persisted.

She shook her head and smiled, and Channing threw Joe a look after which Barthelmess sat down and became quiet.

Janie Ford was about five feet and two inches tall, weighed close to a hundred and fifteen pounds, and it was very attractively arranged, if not attractively displayed, in the loose, belted fawn-dress she wore. Her eyes were dark blue, her hair was honey-blonde. Channing, thinking back to several allusions to her as a child, let his breath out in a silent, regretful sigh; children, in his day, had never, never looked like this.

He lit a cigarette, tossed aside the pack and said, using his nicest smile and softness voice, 'I visited your father this morning.'

'Yes, I know. That's why I'm here. I telephoned him from the University. He told me.' She stopped, leaving both detectives hanging.

'It was just a routine visit,' said Channing, seeking to draw her out again.

She smiled at him. 'Inspector, you're very wise.'

Barthelmess's eyes popped wide open and Channing didn't dare look at him as he smiled, reddening slightly. 'Just a cop,' he said.

She wasn't convinced. 'Psychologically speaking, you have developed a sympathetic, very kindly manner. I doubt if people ever completely avoid being drawn to you when they're in trouble. You have the look of an understanding person. Of course that's part of the cultivated ethos, isn't it?'

Channing's eyes twinkled. 'I don't dare answer that until you tell me what an ethos is.'

She smiled and Channing chuckled at

70

that. Joe Barthelmess's look of surprise crumpled. He laughed aloud. Afterwards, the atmosphere was much easier.

Janie said, 'I knew you'd want to talk to me sooner or later, Inspector Channing, and I didn't want it to happen around my father.'

'Oh?' said Channing, perking up.

'I don't want him upset any more than is necessary.'

'Then we can talk here.'

'Fine. I'll answer any questions.'

She was calmer, more confident now, so Channing decided to spoil that. He said, 'Did you know that you inherit more than a million dollars worth of very valuable income property from Doctor Spence?'

It was a real blow. She blinked, then got pale, and finally she shook her head as though too stunned to speak.

Channing went on. 'Mrs Spence gets the estate, all the cash, bonds, negotiables, things like that, but none of the income property. Not even the clinic — or am I wrong about the clinic, Joe?'

Barthelmess, watching Janie, shook his

head without speaking.

Channing turned back and watched the surprise pass, to be replaced by something else he couldn't define, but which made Janie blush violently. In his cynical secret mind he had a disillusioning thought. There *was* an affair.

'We were friends,' she said, finally, in a slightly hurried tone of voice, 'but he never mentioned anything like that. I don't know what to say. Are you quite sure, Inspector?'

Channing turned again to Joe and Barthelmess nodded at Janie. 'According to Doctor Spence's attorney that's about how the estate will be divided. Miss Ford? People don't give away something worth a million dollars simply because they don't know what to do with it.'

She looked quizzically at Barthelmess. 'Would you explain that, please?'

Channing cut in quickly. 'Tell us about Doctor Spence. What kind of a man was he, for instance; what did you two talk about?'

She was slow taking her eyes off Joe Barthelmess, but when she had, when she was looking at Channing again the little smouldering spark in the depths of her eyes, flickered out. She had guessed what Joe had been driving at. Afterwards, she scarcely looked at Barthelmess at all, and directed everything she said to Channing.

'Well, he was friendly. He helped me set up my schedule at the University for next semester. He seemed particularly interested in my Major, which is psychology. He even said once there was a good field for qualified people in the field of geriatrics, which was his speciality.'

'Did he finance your schooling, by any chance?'

'Not a dime. He didn't offer and I wouldn't have accepted.'

'What kind of an impression did he make on you,' asked Channing. 'I mean, with your basic understanding of psychology, behaviour, all that.'

She thought a moment then said, 'He was vain, and yet in another sense he wasn't vain. If that doesn't make much sense let me put it this way: Doctor

Spence was a man who needed approval, but mostly from himself about himself. He wasn't an insecure person, but he had underlying doubts about his abilities. I rather believe he got into geriatrics because it isn't as complicated a field as, say, neurosurgery or something like that, for which he'd probably didn't think he was qualified, but which he'd never have admitted to anyone, and certainly not to himself. So he was vain in that respect. But off by himself, away from his clinic, his patients, even his wife, he was simply a man who had no outside interests, so when they came along — my schedule at the University, for example — he was frank about his ignorance and his doubts. He never once tried to act like he knew more than he did. We used to have some good laughs together.'

Channing digested all this and said, 'Did he ever mention his wife?'

'Why yes, quite often in fact. He loved her, but I don't think either of them had the ability to give completely. He had his inferiorities to inhibit him.'

'And she?' pressed Channing, getting interested.

'Well, I've only talked to her a few times. My guess — and that's all it can be — is that she'd been very badly burned sometime and this inhibited her. She can't let down, open up, give freely.'

Barthelmess sat back, lit a cigarette and threw a sardonic glance at Channing. But he said nothing.

Janie looked at Channing. 'I'm really not qualified, Inspector . . . '

'I think you've done beautifully,' said Channing. 'Now — dare I risk a very personal question?'

She jumped the gun on him the way everyone else seemed to do when he got skirting around this ticklish question. Still looking him squarely in the eye, although she got a pale shade of pink, she said, 'The answer, Inspector, is — No!' Then she said, 'I don't mean you can't ask the personal question. I mean the answer to it is No! He was friendly, even good company, but he never made a pass and if he had I'd have rejected it immediately.'

'You're sure that's what I was going to ask?' said Channing.

'I'm sure, Inspector. You're clever and smooth and very very good at your line of work. But you are still a detective — and a *man*.'

Channing grinned with approval in spite of himself and Joe Barthelmess, squelched earlier for making a broad innuendo, smiled too. Janie didn't smile. Neither did she look away.

Channing said, 'I believe you. Now, tell me something: Who killed Doctor Spence?'

'I could answer better if you'd ask who *didn't* kill him. Not my father, not his wife, not the maid or the handyman, and not I.'

'That leaves his nephew, Doctor Linden, and a number of John Does — a number of unknowns.'

Janie gave a little start. 'Not Doctor Linden,' she said, and turned scarlet as the pair of detectives sat there blankly regarding her without speaking.

She rose. 'I wish I could help you more, Inspector.'

Channing and Barthelmess also stood up. Joe reached to hold the door. He would like to have been able to make amends but it wasn't going to work out that way and he knew it.

'You've helped,' said Channing, strolling out into the cool cement corridor with Janie. 'And I'm sure if you think of anything else you'll let us know.' He smiled. 'Janie, I'm happy for you about the inheritance.'

She surprised him. 'I can't accept it, Inspector. It belongs to Mrs Spence. I'll stop by on my way home and tell her I can't accept it.'

Channing stood in the corridor watching the very pretty girl walk towards the lift. Then he went back into the room where Joe Barthelmess shoved the door closed and said, 'I believe her, Bob. There *wasn't* an affair.'

Channing threw a cynical look back. 'Okay. I believe her too. And have you any idea what that does? It kills any little chance we had to find a reason for Spence getting knocked off.'

Channing went to his desk, picked up

the cigarette packet and said, 'I'd give a month's pay to be able to listen in when she tells Maude Spence she won't accept that million-dollars worth of property. If I knew what Maude's reaction would be, I'd know whether Maude's our next suspect or not.'

Barthelmess said, with a hung head, '*Someone* better be, because all we've come up with so far is a big fistful of nothing!'

7

The Helpful Flaws

'It was pretty obvious,' Barthelmess told Channing near day's ending. 'Janie's got something going with Will Linden.'

Channing accepted that with indifference. 'They'd make a nice pair — couple of babes in the woods. He's never been anywhere and she'll never go anywhere.'

Channing wanted to stop off at the Moorish house before sundown if he could make it. He had in mind going to see John Harding and, if it were possible, seeing the maid as well.

Channing knew from experience that given a couple of weeks, people close to crimes came up with things; recollections, deductions, fragments, surmises. He wanted to test that notion on the servants at the Spence estate.

Barthelmess said he would wait around

for whatever might come through on the feelers he had out, particularly the one on Carter Spence.

The afternoon was pleasant as Inspector Channing drove through it. Traffic, which would be unpleasant an hour later when the aircraft and other factories changed shifts, was relatively light, the heat was minimal, there was a great rusty smear across the horizon where the sun was bleeding, and the salt-scent was stronger today from the direction of the sea.

By the time Channing reached the Spence place there were a few shadows. It was still springtime; not for another six weeks would summer arrive, and although the heat would be greater, the primary difference was that the days would be longer. Today, there was a hint of this, but also, there was the hint as well of an earlier dusk.

Channing parked out front of the house as he always had, saw Maude Spence open the door as though she'd been watching him approach from the wrought-iron gate back at the entrance to the grounds, and Channing nodded.

She came through, eased the door closed behind, then came down and across to where Channing waited, watching her. She was wearing a white knitted suit trimmed in dark gold. It was plain. It was also obviously very expensive. Her hair, dark and beautifully coiffed, shone with the last rays of daylight. She said, 'Good evening, Inspector. It seems that you never rest.'

He was pleasant. 'I'm probably intruding. I wanted to have another word with Harding and Martin.'

She stopped, gazing up into his face. 'By all means.'

'It won't interfere with dinner, or something like that?'

'Not at all. Would you like me to show you where Harding's quarters are?'

'Thank you, no. At the end of the garage?'

She nodded. 'Inspector, I had a visitor this afternoon. But she said she'd already mentioned to you she'd be stopping by to see me.' The beautiful grey eyes reflected faint irony. 'She told me she would not accept Doctor Spence's bequest.'

Channing nodded. 'I know. That's also what she said at my office.'

'Would you like to know what I told her, Inspector? That she was foolish, inexperienced, impractical and ridiculously idealistic. I wasn't very nice to her was I?'

He didn't know. 'You were forthright at any rate. I suppose all this was said in the nature of giving a young girl good, practical, hard-headed advice?'

'Certainly it was.'

They stood gazing at one another, Channing interested, Mrs Spence hard and defiant. He smiled. 'Did she take the excellent advice?'

'No. Would you have expected her to?'

He smiled. 'No. Although I'm not much of an authority on young women.' He looked at his watch, said he would be as brief as possible with her servants, excused himself and left her standing out there in the lovely evening.

His original idea had been to talk to Harding first, then to the maid. Now he reversed that process because the maid would have dinner to get for her mistress and the handyman would have nothing to do after sundown.

Mary Martin was mousy, alert, well-co-ordinated without being very well constructed, and although on the thin, undistinguished side, she seemed to Channing to possess an ability for noticing things. When he appeared in the kitchen she was surprised, evidently, but beyond that showed no more than the usual degree of discomfort Inspector Channing's presence usually occasioned.

He put her at her ease. He had that knack, as Janie Ford had suggested, and also as Janie had suggested, Channing had worked out the means for appearing a good deal less dangerous than he actually was.

He talked to Mary Martin as she went about her domestic duties in the kitchen, encouraging her to do this. She answered easily, after a bit, feeling adequate in her familiar surroundings, doing familiar things.

She had of course thought of little else but the doctor's slaying, she told

Channing. He had not been a man she admired greatly, he was too conceited round the house, too vain before mirrors, and too condescending towards the hired help, but she was stumped over his murder.

She had not said any of this before when Channing had spoken to her, so he felt it a worthwhile idea, driving out to talk to her. 'Who could have got inside the house so easily that night?' he asked.

'Oh, almost anyone, I expect. But as I told you before, whoever he was, he didn't ring the bell.'

'Where were you after dinner that night?'

'Right here where I'm standin' now.'

'You didn't leave the room even for a few moments?'

'No. I was right here all the while after dinner. No one rang the doorbell, I can tell you that, Inspector.'

'Where was Mrs Spence?'

Mary Martin hesitated but only for a moment. 'She was out back in the yard.'

'Did you see her out there?'

'No.'

'Then how can you know she was out there?'

'She told me the next morning.'

Channing stepped over near the dual sink and gazed out the windows. There was an excellent view of the rear garden. Of course it had been somewhat later, the night of the killing, therefore darker. He stepped back again.

'Mary, for a week or so prior to the murder, who came calling at night?'

She rinsed her hands at the sink, dried them and went to a tall wall-cupboard for dishes as she answered. 'Doctor Linden from the clinic, several other doctors from Westwood — they came with their wives for dinner — that stooped old man who minds the properties, and that's all I can recall.'

Channing was hoping for something better; she'd told him the identical things the first time he'd interviewed her. Then she said, 'There was someone else, only he didn't really come to the house.' She shot Channing a sly look, lowered her head and resumed putting plates from the cupboard upon the kitchen table. 'He drove up down by the gate. I saw the headlamps. Then he backed off, turned and drove away. We have that happen now and then — people curious to see where the road goes, come to the gate and turn back.'

Channing waited. He could tell there was more coming. He could also tell Mary was relishing this. She finished with the plates and began fussing among pots at the stove, her back to him.

'It was a bit after dinner, fairly dark out.' Mary turned suddenly looking squarely at Channing. 'Do you smoke, Inspector?' He nodded. Mary looked disappointed. 'Well, to folks who don't smoke, like the doctor and Mrs Spence and me, when someone comes round who's been smoking, a non-smoker picks up the smell immediately.'

Channing nodded. He thought he knew what was coming.

'When Mrs Spence walked past me in the kitchen just before she went through into the front of the house and found her husband murdered, she smelt very strongly of cigarettes.'

Channing, deciding this could go on forever, cut it short with a question, 'In other words, you think Mrs Spence and the car that pulled up down at the gate were involved some way? Maybe it was a man in the car — someone who smoked — and after the headlamps appeared down there, possibly as a signal, she ducked and went to meet him.'

Mary got plainly uneasy, hearing it put like that, but she nodded. Then she picked up some plates and started past Channing. 'You've got to excuse me, Inspector; I'm a bit behind with supper as it is.' She fled out into the dining-room.

He stood thoughtfully for a moment. Of course, if he reproached the maid she would use the kind of excuse her type of person invariably fell back on: 'You asked who came calling that night, and this person didn't actually come calling at all; he never even came through the gates.'

He wasn't very interested in Mary Martin anyway.

As he left the kitchen by the rear door and paused in the rear garden before heading down for Harding's quarters, he thought Mrs Spence's alibi — being in the garden where she hadn't been able to hear the doorbell — perhaps had more truth in it than she'd intended, for if she were outside the estate, down the road meeting someone, she most certainly couldn't have heard the bell.

Channing ambled down towards Harding's quarters, hands rammed deep into trouser pockets, shoulders, bowed, head down. Had the cold-blooded doctor's widow fooled them all; did she actually have a lover she was meeting? If so, she either picked a very awkward night for her last rendezvous, or perhaps she wasn't as totally baffled by the doctor's death as she seemed to be.

John Harding looked amazed at the identity of his evening caller. He stood back for Channing to enter the small parlour, speechless.

Harding's quarters were very comfortable. Apart from the little sitting-room, there was also a bedroom, a bath, and even a small kitchen. Harding was evidently supposed to be independent of the main house and kitchen. There was a pot of coffee brewing that smelt very good, but when Harding offered Channing a cup the inspector declined.

He asked essentially the same questions he'd asked Mary Martin and up to a point Harding's answers were the same. Where they differed was where Channing hinted at that unknown visitor who'd only flashed his lights at the gate then had driven on. Harding knew nothing of any such event, although he did say those things were fairly common.

Actually, Harding did not say any more than he'd said at his first interrogation directly after the murder. If anything, he seemed more collected now, but he also seemed infinitely more careful. Channing had no trouble arriving at the reason for this but he did not mention it; there was no point in bullying the man over his prison term. If an occasion arose later for this to have a bearing on Channing's investigation, it could be brought forth at that time.

Harding said only one thing that stuck in Channing's mind. The day of the murder he remembered that Mrs Spence had used the telephone in his quarters. It was a minor thing. He'd forgot all about it until now.

Channing asked if she often did this and Harding shook his head. 'Only a couple of times before that I know of.'

'That you know of?'

'Well; she's got keys to everything round here, you know, and there are times when I'm down by the gate, or over in the flowers north of the house when I couldn't see if anyone come in here or not.'

Channing studied the man. Harding had the expression of an alert but weak and mildly troubled individual. Channing did not believe he would deliberately protect Mrs Spence. He was, in fact, tempted to ask Harding's personal and private opinion of her, but refrained because it was getting along in the evening, also because what Harding had inadvertently said, buttressed what Mary Martin had already told Channing, and now he had something more interesting to mull over than the personal assessments of a gardener.

He left Harding and strolled back round to his car. There were lights on in the house now, although it was still fairly bright out.

He wondered which upstairs dressing-room belonged to Maude Spence, and he also wondered how she would react to being accused to having secretly met a man — at least 'he' smoked and met women after dark so it *probably* was a man.

Climbing into his car, Channing lit a cigarette of his own. It was quite an aid to his intellectual process at that. He smiled as he drove out of the grounds heading towards Santa Monica, downhill towards the unseen sea. At last he was beginning to find the little flaws that had to occur in every murder case.

8

A Solid Revelation

Joe Barthelmess was pleased with Channing's revelation the next morning, but he said if Mrs Spence was clandestinely meeting a man — a lover — there would certainly have to be more to it than that.

'Too cold, Bob,' he explained. 'Too untouchable.'

Channing had eaten dinner in his bachelor flat the evening before thinking of the angles that might be involved, so he had also thought of this one. He said, 'There would be more to it. You're right on that point, Joe. But we need this chap's identity.'

'Sweat it out of Mrs Spence,' exclaimed practical and direct Joe Barthelmess.

Channing was more subtle. 'She wouldn't tell us a damned thing.'

Barthelmess threw up his arms. 'Then

who can? You said it happened after dark and only one person saw the headlamps. If Mrs Spence doesn't come through we're shot down.'

Channing reached for the enormous and limp city telephone directory, looked up a name, traced out an address and telephone number which he silently transcribed to a piece of paper, then put the book aside and handed Barthelmess the note.

'Tommy Engels,' he said. 'Her first husband. If I'm wrong I won't break out in tears.'

Joe studied the slip of paper with a gradually clearing face. He arose reaching for his hat. 'I'll find out.'

After Barthelmess had gone Inspector Channing was visited by Gerald Wheaton, from the University. They went out to coffee together and Channing brought Wheaton up to date on the Spence murder. Wheaton, who said the case had dragged on into its third week, gave his opinion as to why the newspapers weren't roasting the police department.

'No one knew Doctor Spence very

well, and those who were acquainted with the man weren't warmed up much by that acquaintanceship. It's in your favour.'

Something else was in Channing's favour; the Malibu hills, ugly, low and brushy knobs actually, dusty, parched, depressing, were burning. It happened every year, thanks no doubt to the pyromaniacal tendencies bound to exist in Los Angel's population of several million people, but ordinarily it occurred later on, during July or August or September when the fire-danger was much greater than it was in late springtime.

As usual, the newspapers were filled with this news. It very conveniently pushed everything else off the front pages.

Wheaton said he'd been digging into Spence's life. 'Not butting in,' he said. 'Just making an evening hobby of it with a view towards seeing that you got all the credit.'

Channing smiled. He wasn't one of those fame-hungry cops. 'Fine with me, Gerry. What did you turn up?'

'The guy sure wasn't an admirable character, was he?'

Channing shook his head, sipped coffee and rummaged for his smokes. He lit one and dropped the pack on the table. Wheaton made no move to take one.

'A number of years ago he came within an inch of being sued by a former patient from whom he'd borrowed a sizeable amount of money.'

Channing hadn't known that, but then he'd been concentrating on other aspects; *living* people, for instance, not dead ones.

'How did it end?' he asked Wheaton.

'Okay, he borrowed enough to get off the hook from his present wife's former husband.'

The cigarette smoke caught in Channing's throat, then he exhaled it, stubbed out the smoke and drained the coffee cup. 'You *have* been digging,' he said.

Wheaton shrugged. 'Fits in, some-how, with her meeting the ex-husband — possibly.'

Channing agreed. 'At least it could have some kind of continuity. Murder so she'd profit and he'd move in with her again. Only . . . '

'Yeah?'

'Gerry, when she mentioned her ex-husband to me she showed the kind of expression a woman who knows how to hate, would show.'

Wheaton wasn't impressed. 'Then the connection has to be different. Suppose she was using him.'

'Is he that naïve?' asked Channing, sounding like he didn't believe it. 'Isn't this guy a professional gambler, a lifetime hardcase?'

'He's that all right. But how do we find out what's inside a man when it comes to something like a beautiful woman he was once married to — and who is now high up in the financial bracket?'

'Barthelmess is doing some checking on him for the night of the murder. I'll keep you informed.'

They parted outside the coffee shop, Wheaton heading for the University, Channing heading for his office, where there was a note saying Doctor Linden had called.

He debated about calling back, decided instead to drive over to the clinic, and did so.

Doctor Linden received Channing in his office. He was brisk, his attitude putting Channing in mind of a person who had something to say he'd have preferred not mentioning.

'It's a matter of ethics,' he said, as his preamble. 'The day Mrs Spence came to the office . . .'

Channing got comfortable in a chair. He didn't offer to help Linden, who was young and serious and uncomfortable, although he could have by simply murmuring a few justifying platitudes.

'Clinical files are not to be removed, Inspector Channing, but the ones on Thomas Engels were taken away. I only made that discovery last evening when I was bringing the records current so that when we have our fiscal audit — for income tax purposes you understand — the books will balance.'

Channing sighed. 'Thomas Engels?' he asked softly.

'A patient of Doctor Spence's who was

with us for a few days last winter.'

Channing said, 'Geriatrics, Doctor Linden?'

'Oh no. Mister Engels wasn't more than perhaps a year or two past forty. It was a lung ailment. Minor one at that. I must say that occasionally we take younger people, but only when they request it.'

'Why would this file disappear?'

Doctor Linden looked up, baffled. 'I can't imagine.'

Channing could imagine but all he said was, 'Anything else, Doctor?'

'No,' muttered Linden, blushing slightly as though he were bothered by what perhaps seemed insignificant to him now. 'That's all. But no one else would have removed the file.'

'You're quite certain of that?'

'Inspector, the files in Doctor Spence's private office were available only to him and to me. There was a clinical copy of all files in our central office. Those were for staff use.' He tapped a Manila folder on the desk. 'This is Mister Engels' file from that room.'

Channing glanced at the folder and Doctor Linden started to hand it over. Channing waved it aside and got to his feet. 'I'm obliged for your co-operation,' he said quietly. 'And Doctor, if you were to consider this a strict confidence between the two of us I'd also appreciate that very much.'

Linden escorted Channing out to his car at the kerbing. He was disturbed that he might have got Mrs Spence into trouble. Channing assured him this probably was not so, but even if it *were* so, she would not discover from Channing where the police had got their information.

It was one of those ambiguous statements policemen are obliged to make, and of course it was true that Channing would not reveal his source, but on the other hand Mrs Spence, who was nobody's fool, wouldn't have to mull things over for long before she knew who — and only who — could have passed this information on to Inspector Channing.

On the drive back to his office Inspector

Channing began to recapitulate all he knew and suspected concerning Maude Spence. He clung stubbornly to his original view, that she was a good hater. If there was something going on between Maude Spence and her one-time husband, he was prepared to aver it was *not* a clandestine romance.

But also he was just as willing to accept the probability that something infinitely more sinister might be involved. Whenever he thought of Mrs Spence he thought of her cold, withdrawn character.

At the office, expecting Joe Berthelmess to be waiting, he found instead that the man filling the chair, waiting, was Carter Spence. The man nodded with only a trace of a smile when Channing entered, and in reply to the question concerning the length of his wait, Spence said, 'Not long, Inspector. Maybe a half hour. It was a shot-in-the-dark, hoping to find you in, but I needed a little time to sort out a few things anyway.'

'For example?' asked Channing, easing down behind the desk and mildly eyeing the big, square-jawed man across from him.

'For example, this doll named Janie. I talked to my uncle's attorney about that estate he left. Why her?'

'What did the attorney say?'

'He didn't know. He said he'd never met her and until he opened the envelope he had no idea what was in the Will.'

'Who drew it up, if your uncle's attorney didn't do it?'

'My uncle. It's legal. It's just a little odd that's all.'

'Because he drew up his own Will?'

Spence seemed to believe Channing was sceptical. He said, 'This same lawyer's been representing my uncle for ten years,' he said defensively. 'He and I both wonder why he didn't have the attorney to draw up those papers.'

Channing wasn't sceptical, he just wasn't too concerned. 'The attorney said it was legal?'

'Yes.'

'Then that is that,' exclaimed Channing. 'As for Janie — she was more surprised than you were when I told her she'd inherited from Doctor Spence. That leaves only one person who'd have any answers for us.'

'Who?'

'Your uncle. And he's dead.'

Carter Spence sat a moment gazing at Inspector Channing. 'But there had to be some reason,' he muttered, 'and it damned well may have to do with his murder.'

Channing didn't dispute that. He did not necessarily believe it either. He had something else in mind at the moment.

Joe Barthelmess came barging in, saw Carter Spence sitting there, and nodded. He then threw a quizzical look towards Channing, tossed aside his hat and said, 'Sure getting hot out.'

Perhaps Spence resented the third person, perhaps he felt something in the air that made him feel like a fifth wheel, in any case he rose, saying, 'Inspector, I'll be around a couple more days, then I've got to get back up north.'

Channing saw him out and afterwards returned to find Barthelmess looking at him with that same quizzical expression.

Joe said, 'What's his trouble?'

'Janie. He's bothered over her inheriting.'

'I thought he wasn't interested in what Spence left behind.'

Channing shrugged. 'He didn't indicate he'd had a change of heart. He just couldn't figure out why Doctor Spence cut the girl in. He also said Spence's Will was drawn up by the doctor himself, not by his attorney.'

Barthelmess saw nothing in that worth mulling over. He said. 'Engels has no alibi for the night Spence was murdered.'

'You got that from a good source, I presume,' said Channing.

Joe smiled. 'The best. From a fink who works for Engels at the nightspot, and who peddles information to the police about the man who pays him. Engels was gone early in the evening, that night, and didn't return to the club until shortly before closing time, which is two-thirty in the morning.'

Channing related to Barthelmess all he'd learned. It tied in very nicely with what Barthelmess had brought back. Joe flopped into a chair and shook a scolding finger at Channing.

'I told you she was my pick for the hand behind the guy who used the knife. Just remember that, Bob I told you at the outset.'

Channing rose, 'What have you got to do this afternoon?'

'Pick up that report on Carter Spence. Why?'

'I'm going back out to have a little heart-to-heart talk with Maude Spence.'

Barthelmess smiled wickedly. 'Careful now, if that woman really wanted to, she could charm the spots off a leopard.'

Channing's eyes shone sardonically. 'But not off an old, scarred tiger.'

'I'll be waiting,' said Barthelmess. 'This ought to put us pretty well along towards an arrest.'

Channing wasn't that optimistic as he strode down to his car. He *hoped* Joe was right, but he was too old a hand at his work to put much faith in those off-hand predictions.

9

A Woman Talks

Maude Spence was doing something Inspector Channing wouldn't have thought she'd ever volunteer for; she was on her hands and knees in a flowerbed, vigorously weeding. She had gloves on, a loose white blouse, and a faded pair of bluejean trousers.

When he drove up she looked as though she'd have fled if there'd been any way to do so. Then she rose, brushed soil from both knees, removed her gloves and came over, neither smiling nor in any way showing that she was self-conscious.

Channing decided to try a touch of friendliness. He said, 'When I was a kid I used to have to do that for my mother. I wondered then and have continued to wonder ever since why it is that weeds will grow profusely where flowers will make only a sickly attempt.'

She still didn't smile but she motioned towards the shade over on the lawn nearer the house, and he strolled along at her side. She said, as they sat down, 'Doctor Spence's nephew telephoned a while ago. He is coming out this evening.' Then she dropped a sentence that solved something for Channing. 'He called a few days ago wanting to come out then, but I wasn't going to be home.'

Channing offered her his packet of smokes. She declined saying she did not use tobacco. She had, but she'd given it up. He lit, considered the burnt match, then dropped it into the packet and returned both to his pocket.

'Mister Engels smokes,' he said, raising mild eyes.

She blinked once, rapidly, but otherwise she didn't move. Channing inhaled, exhaled, leaned back to give her a moment to have bad presentiments, then spoke again.

'Did the three of you know each other, years ago, Mrs Spence?'

She was pale now, her grey eyes focusing on Channing with sudden respect — and sudden fear. She nodded but she did not answer aloud.

'And Doctor Spence, in a little financial difficulty, borrowed money from Mister Engels?'

'Yes.'

Channing kept mildly staring. He held the cigarette in his fingers now. She was badly jarred. He knew she was trying to guess how much Channing actually knew. He meant to enlighten her, but in his own way and in his own sweet time.

'Did the doctor pay Mister Engels back?'

'Every dime.'

'You were married to Engels at the time?'

'Well — no. We were married after Doctor Spence got the loan.'

'Then you knew the doctor?'

'Inspector,' she said, looking indignant at last. 'Don't play cat and mouse with me. If you have something to say — say it!'

Channing obliged. 'What did he want when you met him the night of the murder — to know whether the knife he'd brought along was better than a pistol?'

She gasped, one hand flying to her lips. 'It was nothing like that at all.'

'What then?' demanded Channing, staring hard and no longer so soft-spoken.

'He . . . '

'You telephoned him earlier,' prompted Channing.

'Yes. I called him from Harding's room. He . . . He'd contacted me last winter. A mutual acquaintance told him I'd married again. She'd seen me with Doctor Spence.'

Channing felt like groaning. He had already jumped ahead to what was coming and it wasn't anything he wanted it to be.

'Tommy telephoned. I met him that first time, in the city for luncheon.'

'What was his proposition?'

She flinched. 'Blackmail.'

Channing put out his cigarette feeling cheated, and also feeling disgusted. He might have guessed but he hadn't.

'Explain please,' he said, resorting to that mild tone again.

'He reminded me of the loan. I told him it had been repaid and he laughed at me. He said he still had the note, that he hadn't ever returned it to Doctor Spence. He also said something else . . . that . . . the reason he'd left me and had got that divorce was because Doctor Spence and I had been having an affair behind his back.'

Channing eased back as he listened, watching the cold, serene features become alive, tormented and twisted. He was almost as fascinated by that as he was by what he was being told.

'There had never been any affair.' She wasn't denying it as much as she was being scornful about such a suggestion. It rang true. 'He knew it, too. But he said between the old note, never marked paid, and the lurid story he'd spread, he could ruin Doctor Spence.'

Channing nodded. It was a very old story but each time he heard it he was struck by the same thought. Nice guy, this.

'He wanted one hundred thousand dollars in cash.'

'A question,' broke in Channing. 'Is Mister Engels in financial difficulties that you know of?'

'Inspector,' she said bitterly, 'Tommy Engels is *never* in financial difficulties. He has more sources of revenue than the police know about.'

'How do you know that, Mrs Spence, if you hadn't seen him in all those intervening years?'

'Because I *know* him, that's how. He is a hustler, a worker. Old friends I've run into now and then have told me how he's climbed up step over step — or should I have said body over body.'

'To the night of the murder, Mrs Spence — why that particular night?'

'I was supposed to give him my answer. Whether I'd buy my husband's reputation from him for a hundred thousand dollars, or whether he'd start ruining Carleton. He gave me a week to telephone him. I put it off to the very last minute. Then I called. He said he'd turn in at the gate, shining his headlights. That would let me know he'd arrived. I was then to go down to the road and meet him.'

'And you did?'

She nodded. 'I told him there just was no way for me to get my hands on one hundred thousand dollars. Not a way in this world.'

'And . . . ?'

'He compromised. He said he knew I could get hold of a thousand dollars a week. That he'd settle for that.'

'One hundred weeks?'

'Yes.'

'You agreed?'

Maude Spence's eyes wavered, then fell. 'Yes,' she whispered.

'Who mentioned murder, Mrs Spence?'

'Neither of us, Inspector. I swear that to you.'

Channing sat in impassive thoughtfulness for a moment. Joe Barthelmess had been so very, very wrong. Worse, not only did it look as though they had come no closer to a murderer, it began to also look as though they were right back where they'd started from.

He said, 'Why did you remove the

Engels file from your husband's office?'

It startled her, but she recovered quickly. 'I didn't want you to find it. I'd told you I hadn't seen Tommy since we were divorced.'

Channing believed that. In fact, that had been his private theory since he'd first learned the identity of the patient whose file had been taken.

'That night,' he said, deliberately speaking slowly. 'Think back to that night, Mrs Spence. You left the house after dinner.'

'Yes.'

'And you walked around the house down to the roadway. Your husband was in his study. Harding was in his quarters. Martin was in the kitchen.'

'Yes.'

'As you approached the gate, someone — a man — either passed you bound towards the house, or he had just gone on by and was probably behind you. Do you remember that?'

Channing was barely breathing as he watched her beautiful eyes cloud over in an effort at recollection. Then she shook her head. 'I'm sorry.'

Channing could have cursed. Instead he tried again. 'Doctor Spence was expecting someone that night. You and he had dinner, as usual, and you talked . . . '

'Inspector, I know what you're trying to do, but it's no use. Carleton and I had dinner but he had something on his mind that night. He was quiet. As you now know, I also had something on my mind. We scarcely even said good evening to one another as we sat down. There was no general conversation at all.'

Channing still would not give up. 'Your husband, as you say, had something on his mind. But it hadn't just popped up that evening, surely. Over the past week, or perhaps the immediately preceding few days, he'd been thinking about something. He mentioned it to you.'

She sighed softly and showed Channing a very faint, whimsical little smile. 'My husband very rarely ever discussed the clinic or his investments with me, Inspector. He was a man of set and ingrained habits. He'd been unmarried a long time when he and I were married. In that long interim he'd established his habits. He hadn't changed them before he was killed. I'm sorry, but whatever was on his mind, he did not mention in front of me.'

'But you're perceptive, Mrs Spence. You knew him, you understood about the clinic, his other affairs, to some extent. Make a calculated guess for me.'

She lowered her head and considered the hands in her lap. For a long moment she was quiet. Then she looked up again.

'Janie.'

Channing nodded. 'What about Janie?'

'Well, that's just it, Inspector. I don't know. For a while I thought it was an affair. He'd meet her at the University and drive her home. He'd go down there once in a while or she'd come here. But it was never a rendezvous. As I told you before, if it'd been anything like that I'd have known it instantly.'

'Mrs Spence,' said Channing. 'Janie's no child. She's every inch a woman.'

The troubled grey eyes conceded this

but would not be shaken from whatever was behind them, in Maude Spence's brain. 'I'd have known, Inspector,' she murmured softly. 'You see, I'm not a girl any longer, and apart from Tommy Engels I've known other men. They're pretty much the same. A woman gets to predict things.' She smiled. 'It just wasn't an affair, you'll have to believe me, Inspector.'

He believed her. He'd believed the same thing before she'd ever put it into words. But that only clouded the issue, it didn't resolve it, and Channing was now well along towards losing the little ground he'd thus far gained.

He made one last attempt, then shifted his tactics. He said, first, 'What did the doctor *say* about Janie?'

'Oh, that he felt sorry for her, having no mother. That she was very bright and he had high hopes for her.' The grey eyes were kindly now. 'Everything a man might say about some youngster he'd taken a shine to.'

Channing went on to his next topic now; there was nothing more to be gained from Maude Spence on the Janie Ford topic.

'Do you realize that Engels is in serious trouble over what you've told me?'

'Yes.'

'Has he tried to see you since the murder?'

'He has telephoned, but I gave Mary word I wouldn't talk to anyone but the police and the lawyers.'

'Do you think he's finished, now that Doctor Spence is dead, or will he continue to threaten you?'

'Inspector,' she said quietly. 'You don't know Tommy Engels, do you?'

Channing shook his head, slapped his knees and rose. 'No. But I expect to know him.' He smiled down at her. 'I had hopes when I drove in here.'

She rose very slowly. She seemed more human now than at any other time he'd seen her. She strolled down to the car with him.

'I wish I could tell you something, Inspector, *anything* at all that would help. But you see, I've had my own troubles all through this thing. The

116

moment I recovered from the shock of seeing Carleton hanging there in that chair, dead, I was petrified. I couldn't even cry for him. I was terrified that Tommy might have done that to frighten me — to break me down. Afterwards, when I had more of a chance to think, I knew it couldn't have been Tommy. My husband never would have allowed him into the house. *Then* something else occurred to me: With Carleton gone I was entirely at Tommy's mercy.'

'There are the police,' said Channing gently. 'Odd thing how people in trouble always think they have to do everything by themselves. Well, I'm sorry I upset you.'

As Channing drove away he flicked on the car's police-band intercom and reached Joe Barthelmess. 'Get a warrant for extortion on Thomas Engels,' he said, 'and pick him up right away.' He didn't say the need for urgency was prompted by a suspicion that Maude Spence, in a weak and maudlin moment, might regret saying so much, and might telephone her former husband to warn him.

10

More Questions, Fewer Answers

Maude didn't warn Engels, for as Joe Barthelmess said when he brought the prisoner in to be booked, the man was sound asleep on a leather sofa in his spacious office at the nightclub when Joe made his appearance.

Engels was a thin-faced, lithely-built man, greying at the temples but smooth-faced and youthful looking, although dissipation had left its mark around the lips and eyes.

When Inspector Channing went to the cell for a talk Engels wasn't especially inflamed. He was indignant about being arrested, booked and locked up, but he was sitting and smoking when Channing came along, and nodded agreeably, if not necessarily pleasantly. He thought the police had a poor charge.

Channing was not so sure. When

Engels said he'd telephoned his attorney, that he'd be out on bail within an hour, Channing said, 'You'll be back. I'll have you locked up again before the arraignment, and afterwards, and every chance I get between now and the trial, and if the jury frees you, Engels, I'll find something else. That's a promise.'

Engels sat gazing through bars at Inspector Channing. Sounding more baffled than surprised about Channing's animosity, he said, 'Inspector, we don't even know each other. What have I done to you? Look, if you lost a little money at a crap game or poker at the club, I'll make it good the minute I'm out of this iron cottage. Where's the rub?'

Channing ignored the statement, lit a smoke of his own and said, 'Spence was too good to pass up, wasn't he; gave you a natural set up, having your former wife married to him?'

Engels stepped on the cigarette he'd been smoking, leaned with both hands behind his head, against the cement wall of his cell and said, 'Carleton Spence was the biggest fake you ever knew in your life, Inspector. Okay, I tried to shake him down through my ex-wife. But murder . . . ? Inspector, that guy was too contemptible. He lied like a trooper, he bilked old people out of their savings, he cheated every way that he knew how. Don't tell me about Spence, I knew the man twenty years or more. I'm the guy he came whining to when he first started out and got into trouble over money. I made a loan and — '

'And thought he was after your wife.'

Engels stopped speaking for five seconds while he carefully studied Inspector Channing's face. It seemed that Engels had suddenly found himself facing a man who knew as much about what had happened those long years ago, as Engels remembered himself.

'I wasn't married to her then,' Engels finally said. 'We were planning on it. As for Spence, he couldn't have competed for her with me anyway. He *thought* he was God's gift to women. He fooled a lot of them too, but he didn't fool me and he didn't go round where Maude was.' Engels shook his head. 'Inspector,

I didn't kill Spence, but I'll tell you this: Whoever *did* kill him deserves a medal. The man was no good inside and outside.'

'But you,' said Channing mildly, 'are suffused with blinding virtue.'

Engels shook his head. 'Got another cigarette?' After Channing had passed his pack through the bars and held a match, Engels exhaled smoke and smiled. 'I'll keep the smokes; kind of hard getting any in here . . . Me?' Engels came to stand on the inside of the bars facing Channing. 'A guy can be a lot of things, Inspector, and as long as he don't lie to himself he'll know where the line is. When he starts making excuses for the lousy things he does, or the illegal things he does, then he's on his way down. Me?' Engels shook his head slowly. 'I'm a hustler. I know it even better than you know it. But I don't judge people. A guy like Spence isn't worth your contempt. I wouldn't dirty my hands stickin' a knife into a guy like Carleton Spence.'

'But you'd blackmail him, Engels.'

'That's different. I'm making him

squirm. That's a laugh to me. But kill him . . . ?' Engels turned, went to the bunk and sat down again. 'I wouldn't even waste the money to hire some punk to knock a guy like Spence off.'

It was both an interesting philosophy that Engels had, and an interesting viewpoint on Doctor Spence. Not that Inspector Channing had expected Engels to say anything very different, but he'd now come face to face with contempt rather than hatred of the defunct doctor from just about everyone he'd talked to.

And of course, although he did not really feel qualified to do it, he made his own judgement, based on all he'd learned, and he too, secretly and privately, held Carleton Spence in contempt.

After he left Engels he encountered Joe Barthelmess and a short, wiry, greying man in the corridor leading from the street-entrance to the central receiving office. Joe flagged Channing down.

'Inspector, this is Mister Greenspan, Engels' attorney. Mister Greenspan, this is Inspector Channing.'

They exchanged a brief handgrip and

the attorney launched into a quick and predictable denunciation. Channing smiled. 'He's all yours Mister Greenspan. Post the bail and take him home with you.'

The attorney cocked his head like a small predatory bird. 'You sound like a cop with a good case, Inspector.'

'Good enough. You'll find out at the preliminary arraignment.'

'Witnesses? Sound violation?'

Channing kept smiling. 'See for yourself when the District Attorney files his charges against Engels.'

'Wait a minute,' said the lawyer as Channing started to turn. 'Extortion?'

'Yes.'

'But the guy's dead — this Doctor Spence.'

'You'd better talk to your client,' said Channing. 'He didn't try extortion against Spence. It was against the doctor's wife, and she's very much alive. Come on, Joe.'

They left the attorney gazing after them.

Pacing slowly along in the direction of

the office, Channing told Barthelmess all that had occurred at the Spence estate earlier. Joe listened with interest. His later comment concerned Engels.

'With his record and with Mrs Spence's testimony, I don't see a jury letting Engels walk away.'

Of course that was one man's hopeful opinion, but as a matter of fact juries were the most thoroughly unpredictable dispensers of legal punishment on earth. At least with judges, especially the irresponsibly liberal ones, of which far too many sat on benches in courtrooms, the police knew what to expect. Not so with juries, particularly juries with very many women on them.

But something else interested Barthelmess even more. 'This doesn't help the main theme though, Bob.'

Channing held the door for Barthelmess to enter the office first. 'Right you are. I recall someone crowing about having everything neatly wrapped up before I went out to have that talk with Mrs Spence.' He closed the door, went behind the desk and sat down.

Barthelmess made a grimace. 'Okay. Wishful thinking. But the thing is — where are we right this minute, if not just about back where we started from?'

'You've guessed it. Right back where we started from.' Channing was regretful. 'And the hell of it is, according to my calculations, at about the time Maude Spence was hastening down across the front of the grounds to meet Engels beyond the damned gate, someone was heading past on up to the house to kill her husband.'

Barthelmess raised his head as though to ask the obvious question and before he could phrase it, Inspector Channing began shaking his head.

'She didn't see anything nor hear anything.'

Barthelmess groaned.

It was past noon and Channing's stomach was reminding him of this fact with little rumbling sounds. He suggested luncheon but Barthelmess had already eaten. He had been on his way back from lunch, in fact, when he'd encountered Greenspan downstairs.

They sat a moment looking at one another, then Channing heaved himself upright out of the chair and said he'd be back after a bit, and departed.

There were any number of restaurants near the police building, which was in a clutch of other civic structures, and Channing actually had no preferences. This time, he entered a French cafe, scarcely conscious of which place he'd chosen, because in the back of his mind something was stirring.

It wasn't entirely a matter of sifting out what he thought might be lies from what he felt might be true, although he believed both Maude Spence and Tommy Engels. At least he believed her *attitude*, which was against violence and favourable to being blackmailed in order to save her husband from a terrible scandal. He also believed Engels' attitude, which was contemptuous of the man he had devised a means for ruining if he couldn't extort a fortune from that man's wife.

And there was no murder in either of those attitudes. It limited the field somewhat, but in another sense it broadened it. Channing ate without conscious effort and afterwards, instead of going back to the office he got his car and drove out to the Spence clinic.

Doctor Linden was making his rounds, Channing was told by the crisp and handsome receptionist. She knew who Channing was and asked him if he'd mind waiting in Doctor Linden's office. He didn't mind at all, and in fact he didn't stop there but went on through to the office of Doctor Spence beyond, and there he glanced through the appointment book, studied the filing cabinets, then began a rather systematic and unauthorized examination of those voluminous records.

He ran across a file on Janie's father, Frank Ford. The man had a bad heart; Doctor Spence had cared for him personally according to his file, and a pacemaker had been installed, one of those little electronic devices that through sequential timing set the pace of the heart's muscular contractions to aid the health and prolong the life of the patient.

It was interesting reading. Channing knew what a pacemaker was but only vaguely understood how the things worked until he read Ford's file.

He also found a file on John Harding, which made him wonder if Doctor Spence made a habit of treating people whom he knew but whose ailments were somewhat outside the doctor's speciality. Normally, Channing knew from experience that specialists usually sent patients whose ailments were outside their special fields, to other specialists or to general practitioners.

There were several other names he encountered that were familiar, but not germane, so he closed the file and sauntered back into Linden's office where he was standing by a window gazing out into an enclosed large patio where several robed people, convalescents from the looks of them, were sunning themselves, reading, or visiting back and forth, when Doctor Linden came in.

The medical man was brisk. 'I'm sorry to have kept you waiting,' he said, putting a metal clipboard on top of the desk and dropping into the chair nearby. 'It's been a little hectic around here lately. One man doing two men's work.'

Inspector Channing was sympathetic. 'Why not bring in another doctor?'

Linden nodded, studying Channing. 'I've made that recommendation to Mrs Spence.'

'She doesn't like it?'

'She said to do whatever I thought necessary. She also said I'd have to clear everything through Janie — Miss Ford.'

Channing digested this with a slight nod. 'The new owner, or partner, or whatever she is, eh?'

William Linden shot his chair forward and leaned upon the desk. 'It isn't pertinent to what interests you, Inspector, but I suppose you ought to know I've been seeing a lot of Miss Ford.'

Inspector Channing wasn't the least bit surprised. He'd deduced something like this since his last meeting with Janie, when she'd sprung to Doctor Linden's defence during a discussion of possible suspects.

'You have good taste,' Channing murmured.

Linden kept watching the detective. He seemed to be trying hard to guess what Channing's *real* thoughts were — which obviously meant he and Janie had discussed Channing between them.

'But it had nothing whatever to do with the clinic,' said Linden, defensively. 'We were engaged before anything happened to Doctor Spence.'

Channing hadn't guessed that but it didn't surprise him. Neither did it particularly interest him. Something else *did* interest him, though. 'Tell me, Doctor, what was Carleton Spence's reaction to this?'

'Well . . . He only knew we were seeing each other. I didn't tell him we were engaged.'

It was the man's shifting glance that gave Channing his clue. 'He didn't like it?'

'He said she was too young to be serious with a man.'

Channing raised his eyebrows. 'Twenty-one is too young?'

Linden nodded. 'That's what he said. We just decided, in order to keep peace, not to mention how things really stood between us. Then he was killed.'

11

'You Can't Win Them All'

Inspector Channing's purpose in visiting the clinic had been to ascertain from Doctor Linden if there were any patients of the late Carleton Spence who might fit the category of good haters.

Being side-tracked by a youthful love affair was diverting; it was even pleasant, but unless it had some bearing on what Channing was seeking — a murderer — he wasn't liable to let it divert him for long. As he'd said, Janie was past the legal age of consent for women, so whatever objections Doctor Spence might have had, unless Linden and the girl were willing to acknowledge them, there hadn't been much Spence *could* do — nor was there much Channing *would* do.

It was just something else that fit into place, and every case Inspector Channing had been on had some of these little diversions for the elemental reason that nothing really changed very much when someone died, in the lives of the people around the victim.

It was this fresh avenue that absorbed Channing at the moment, for having lost several suspects, or at least having discovered they were unlikely murderers, he wanted substitutes, because somewhere along the way he was going to lock onto the real killer if he persevered, and there was one thing no one ever took away from Robert Channing: He persevered.

But Doctor Linden wasn't too helpful. In fact, he seemed reluctant to go into this matter. Channing thought he understood why: After all, Linden had been working with, and for, Doctor Spence for several years. He would also know the kind of man Spence was, at least professionally, and it wasn't very difficult to see Linden as one of those highly ethical, idealistic young men to whom any form of cheating was anathema.

Channing made it a little easier by

saying, 'Look, Doctor, I suppose I've heard enough about Doctor Spence by now not to be greatly surprised by anything you can add. But angel or devil, the fact that he was murdered remains. I'm fairly confident he had detractors among his patients. After all, even if he'd been a paragon of virtue, having practised medicine for a quarter century or longer, he'd have enemies, wouldn't he?'

Linden agreed, but not cheerfully. 'He was a complex person, Inspector. He did what we all do: charged according to what he thought the traffic would bear. After all, America doesn't have socialized medicine you know, and doctors have a good deal of leeway. On the other hand, in his defence, I can tell you of any number of cases where he worked without any pay whatsoever.'

It was the oldest argument in the lexicon of medical arguments. Gouging one patient was justified because another patient was treated *gratis*. Of course it was an innocuously childish contention by itself, but when one considered how immensely rich medical practitioners became within a few years of entering private practice, one was perfectly justified in believing not many *gratis* patients were actually treated, relatively speaking.

Channing said, with a faint hint of irony, 'I'm sure he was a Good Samaritan, Doctor. But about the ones he treated who reacted ungratefully . . . '

Linden's brow furrowed. If Janie had been there she might have said her fiancée was trying to recall something with one part of his brain, that the other part did not want recalled. Finally, however, he said, 'Well, there was of course this man Engels. The one whose file Mrs Spence removed.'

'He was ungrateful?'

'It was more than that, Inspector. He insisted, after each visit by Doctor Spence, that I examine him too. He didn't trust Doctor Spence.'

Channing could understand that. 'Anyone else?' He didn't mention that Engels was in police custody.

'Well, there were any number of cranks. In geriatrics you must expect that. Elderly people with ailments that affect both disposition and outlook, rarely respond to the payment of medical bills with enthusiasm.'

Channing inwardly sighed. He wasn't going to be too successful at pinning Linden down to specific names and details, that was obvious. He took a shot in the dark.

'Harding, for example, Doctor. Was he a disgruntled patient?'

Linden gazed at Channing with fresh respect. 'You don't miss very much do you, Inspector. As a matter of fact John Harding was one of the grateful ones. His trouble, as you may know, stems mostly from nervous disorders, the result of prolonged suffering during the Korean War.'

'Frank Ford, Doctor?'

Linden considered his hands which were clasped on top of the desk. 'Not an easy man to assess, Inspector, because he is very quiet, very unobtrusive. I would say that somewhere in his life tragedy has hit him very hard. But as for being a patient, he was a good one.'

'His relationship with Doctor Spence . . . ?'

'Good, as far as I know. While he was here — there was corrective surgery for a heart condition — he said very little, was an exemplary patient, and was liked by staff and the patients.'

Channing persevered doggedly. 'Doctor, tell me the name of one outstanding patient, who did not like Doctor Spence.'

'We had a man named Roger Chaney two years ago who sticks out in my mind as the most likely person for your cause, Inspector. He was in his early sixties, had been a building contractor, was rough and big and very irritable. He had prostate trouble — very common I'm sure you know, in men of that age. Doctor Spence performed the operation, successfully of course, since he'd performed thousands just like it, and everything went along fairly well, although Chaney growled and swore at everyone, until the day he was to be discharged. It's clinic policy to present the bill for payment at that time. Chaney hit the ceiling.'

'He'd been charged on that basis you mentioned a moment ago, I take it,' murmured Channing, and Linden could discern the disapproval in the words as well as the voice.

'Inspector, Mister Chaney was a very wealthy man . . . Yes, he was charged according to our sliding scale. He swore we'd have to sue to get a dime of it. He called me a pup and he called Doctor Spence a dishonest sawbones who robbed the elderly — among other things. He even said he'd see Doctor Spence in hell if he had to send him there himself.'

Channing finally had one name. He considered young Doctor Linden, then asked a question. 'Did you people sue?'

'Yes. We had to.'

'Did suing patients bother Doctor Spence?'

Linden looked away then back. 'It didn't.'

'But it bothered you?'

'Well, not with someone like Roger Chaney, but with some of the others.'

'And among those others, Doctor, was there another good hater?'

Linden threw up his hands. 'I suppose so. We've handled any number of patients here. Santa Monica, you undoubtedly realize, has been the retirement town for elderly people for a great many years.'

Channing rose. 'I'll look up Mister Chaney,' he said, 'and if you think of any others I'd appreciate a call.'

Doctor Linden seemed enormously relieved that the visit was terminating. He went out into the shiny, quiet corridor with Inspector Channing. As they walked side-by-side towards the front exit they were met, and nodded to, by several shuffling elderly men. They also saw three crisp nurses and Channing asked how large the staff was.

'Fifteen fulltime people,' answered Doctor Linden, and smiled. 'Plus one practitioner. Pretty lopsided percentage, I'd say.'

Outside, the afternoon was well advanced but it wasn't as hot as it might have been. Channing thanked Doctor Linden and departed. On the drive back to his office he had a conviction that this had been one of his more disappointing and unproductive days.

But he was philosophical. In other

instances, following other leads and investigating other felonies, he'd marked time between leads and arrests for a lot longer than one day, or one week, if the facts were known.

Joe Barthelmess was waiting although it was five o'clock — quitting time — when Channing reappeared at his office, which proved that police work, unlike most other lines of individual endeavour, kept its active people too engrossed most of the time to bother with clock-watching.

Barthelmess finally had a revised and up-to-date rundown on Carter Spence. He looked a little anticipatory, a little baffled. 'The guy's valour was never in question, but reading between the lines of this official report I get the distinct impression his common sense from his own wartime experience, 'means dereliction for duty. Drunk at his post. Otherwise the military record's all right.'

'Ten years in anyone's army,' said Channing, speaking from his own war-time experience, 'means dereliction for anyone. But only the dumb ones get caught. Anything else?'

'An old assault and battery charge in a bar-room brawl. Eight years back.'

'I can believe that too,' said Channing, dropping down at the desk and reaching for the telephone. 'One look at Spence would tell you, under the right combination of circumstances, he'd break up a lot of furniture.'

Channing dialled, got someone, and said, 'This is Inspector Channing. I'd like whatever you have in the records concerning a man named Roger Chaney. I would make his current age at about sixty-five or thereabouts, his former occupation contractor, his present status retired. Yes, in Santa Monica although he may have lived in L.A. as well. I'll be waiting.'

As Channing rang off Joe Barthelmess looked at him. 'Who is Roger Chaney?'

Channing replied with feeling more than fact. 'Will-o-the-wisp, I think. Someone Doctor Linden recalls as being virulently opposed to Doctor Spence.' He grinned. 'Joe, we've wasted a perfectly good day.'

Barthelmess nodded, tossed the report

on Carter Spence atop Channing's desk and said, 'Yeah. Even Engels is gone.' He yawned and looked at his watch. 'You can't win 'em all.'

After Joe had decided to call it a day and had gone, Channing continued to sit at his desk, a lean, tanned, curly-headed buddha in quiet reflection. When the telephone rang an hour later he reached for it.

The report on Roger Chaney was interesting. It was also terminal. The man had indeed fought a legal skirmish with Spence over a clinic bill. He had indeed made a number of very strong accusations against Spence. In fact everything William Linden had said was correct, but much milder than the facts as turned up by the Records and Files Section people, who were very efficient at their work.

But the most illuminating of all that Inspector Channing was told was the verified fact that Roger Chaney had died three years ago in a Montrose private hospital, after moving away from Santa Monica.

Channing replaced the telephone.

A man dead three years couldn't have murdered a man dead one month.

Channing rose, ran a set of bent fingers through his hair and went to the lone window in his office to watch dusk settle in.

Down where the traffic never ceased running, streetlamps were coming on, shadows were thickening between rows of buildings, and storefronts flickered with neon brilliance in every conceivable colour and shade.

Channing repeated to himself what he'd said to Joe Barthelmess: This had been a wasted day. But he wasn't the least bit downcast. In fact, as he turned to get his hat and leave the building, he was already wondering if there might not be a worthwhile motion picture at one of the neighbourhood theatres. His taste ran to simple things without any physical stresses. His favourite movie producer was Walt Disney Studios.

Maybe the majority of human beings needed vicarious amusement; indeed to revel in the emotional disturbances of all manner of psychotic actors, on screen and off, but Inspector Channing, who lived it every day with people he investigated, didn't need it.

It was a beautiful evening out, by the time he got to his car. Just for a moment he thought of Maude Spence. It would be nice sitting outside in the gloaming talking with her, he thought, and got into his car, started the engine — and drove straight home to his own flat.

12

A Matter of Doubt

Carter Spence was back the next morning with an interesting suggestion. He had, he told Inspector Channing, before Joe Barthelmess arrived to listen in, been doing some research on his uncle, and his aunt-in-law with whom he'd spent an unrewarding hour the previous evening.

'The guy was a skirt-chaser twenty years back, and he caught a few, so I was told by people who used to know him, and there were some of those broads who afterwards had plenty of reason to hate him. Now I'm wondering if one of those women didn't do him in?'

Channing was bland. 'No. We have the Coroner's word for it that someone with great strength, even for a man, would have to have run that knife into Doctor Spence the way it was done.'

'Okay. Then one of these women had a

lover or husband, or something like that, who would do the job for her.'

Channing couldn't refute this as a possibility, although he very much doubted it as a fact. Then Joe arrived looking rosy-cheeked and fresh, and Carter Spence cocked a jaundiced eye at him.

'Look, Barthelmess,' said the big man, 'if there's anything you want to know about me — come to me for the answers.'

Barthelmess was in a good mood, doubtless still savouring a pleasant breakfast and driving through the lovely morning; he couldn't be antagonized. As he dropped into a chair he nodded agreeably. 'All right. What makes you think I'm interested in you?'

'You went nosing around among people I used to know when I lived down here. I got a couple of telephone calls last night.'

Inspector Channing didn't like Spence's attitude. 'We have work to do,' he said quietly, looking squarely at Spence. 'You don't have to like how we do it, but you'd better hope it pays off because otherwise not just the person who killed your uncle, but a lot of other killers, won't get picked up.'

Spence had no ill feelings towards Channing, evidently, because he shrugged his great shoulders, shot Joe another, final, unpleasant glare, then returned to his former subject by saying, 'What about this other angle, Inspector?'

Channing felt like swearing. There was just one thing worse than a difficult felony; that was well-meaning amateurs horning in to help solve it. He said, 'We'll consider it. If there's any merit I'll let you know.'

Spence was no novice, he knew a brush-off when he heard one. But he wasn't quite ready to leave yet either, for he now said, 'Something else, Inspector, that guy Linden who worked for my uncle has the hots for that Janie Ford.'

Channing felt mildly resentful. 'I am aware of that,' he said, seeking with brusqueness to get this interview over with.

'Okay, so you're aware of it. Did you also know Linden had dinner last night with Maude Spence and afterwards they went for a drive in the country — under a nearly full moon?'

This implication kept both Barthelmess and Channing staring at burly Carter Spence so long, in total silence, that eventually the burly man squirmed in his chair, then spoke on.

'After I left her, last night, I was drivin' back down the lane in my rented car, when this flashy black sports car passes me. Like I said, there was a big moon. I recognized the guy driving as Doctor Linden.'

'So you parked somewhere out of sight,' said Channing, 'and waited.'

Spence scowled. 'Something wrong with that?'

Channing shrugged without answering. If there was anything wrong with it he was certain Spence would never agree with what a policeman might think.

'I sat there an hour and a half before they came along, in the black sports car with Linden driving. I had my car down a little lane but I had walked back up to stand near some trees not very far from the Spence gate. They had to go slow as they left the estate and turned down the roadway. I distinctly heard her say to him, 'There is nothing to worry about, Will. It's all going very well'.'

Joe Barthelmess moved his lips as though repeating these words for their savour. Inspector Channing kept looking at Carter Spence. 'You couldn't have been mistaken?'

'They weren't a hundred feet away, it was a still night, the car hadn't gained speed after leaving the gate and making the turn, Inspector. I was *not* mistaken.'

Barthelmess pushed up in his chair and said, 'They aren't altogether incriminating words, Mister Spence. Maybe she simply meant everything was going very well from the standpoint of the clinic.'

'Or,' said Spence sardonically, 'from the standpoint of a murder not getting solved.'

Channing thought and said nothing. One thing surprised him; the implication of intimacy. It didn't jibe at all with what he knew of the people involved, and that set him to thinking. If Doctor Linden and Maude Spence were close, then perhaps there had been something like that going on while she was still married to Doctor Spence. Also, by Linden's own account he was in love with Janie Ford. Why would he then take his former employer's beautiful widow for a moonlight drive, evidently so they could have a private discussion, if not something else?

Channing moved back to the time before Linden had arrived at the Spence estate, to the hour Carter Spence had spent with the widow. He said, 'What did you and Mrs Spence talk about?

Spence acted like a man recalling something that didn't please him as he said, 'The murder, primarily. Then the business of Janie Ford inheriting. She got mad.'

Channing could visualize that without much effort; Carter Spence was not a man who would be notorious for tact.

'I told her I'd already told the attorney representing my uncle's estate I didn't want anything for myself. I also told her that this gave me the right to be a little sceptical of the others.'

'Like Janie?' murmured Channing.

'Yes, like Janie. I said it all had a bad smell to me. Not just Janie's part in it, but the part of everyone else, too. That's when she got mad.'

Joe Barthelmess was regarding the big man with a kind of sardonic amusement. As though he were amused that anyone could be as dense as Carter Spence made himself appear at this sitting.

'She asked me to leave, finally,' said Spence, 'so I pulled out. That's when I saw Linden. That's also when it hit me why she was so anxious to get rid of me. Because she didn't want me to see him coming round.'

Inspector Channing was beginning to share the feelings of Joe Barthelmess but he concealed it better. Arising, he said, 'This has all been very interesting, and believe me we'll look into it. But I want you to promise me something: No more detective work, Mister Spence.'

The big man stood up. 'Why not? You guys don't seem to be making much progress.'

'Don't *seem* to be,' said Channing, 'is a lot different than not *making* progress.

151

We're getting along. For example, the only thing you've said this morning, or hinted at, that we haven't already discovered, is that bit about Mrs Spence and Doctor Linden going car-riding. And that's no crime no matter what either of them said. But we'll look into that too.' Channing blandly smiled. 'We're not ingrates, but sometimes the best intentions under the sun do more harm than good.'

Channing saw Spence out into the corridor, then returned to where Joe Barthelmess was lighting a cigarette. As he flipped the match Joe said, 'I'd hate to be under that guy in the army, or have to work for him on some construction job.'

Channing wasn't concerned with Spence's personality. He stood beside the desk and said, 'It doesn't ring true, Joe. Either Spence misunderstood, or we've let something escape us. If Linden plans to marry Janie, why would he be moonlight-riding with Maude?'

Barthelmess blew smoke, crossed his legs, leaned back and said, 'Don't *ask* me,

Inspector, I'm just a low-grade detective. *Tell* me.'

Channing couldn't. He hadn't worked out the options yet. He picked up his hat, dropped it on the back of his head and said, 'I guess I'd better go find out, hadn't I? Want to ride along?'

Barthelmess was comfortable. 'No thanks. I'll stay here and pray for you.'

They parted grinning at one another, and by the time Inspector Channing got to his car he was wondering exactly how he could quote those words to Maude Spence without getting about the same reaction Carter Spence had got the night before when he'd made some crude reference to Janie and Carleton Spence.

But he had ample time to thresh that out on the drive to the knoll, which lay westerly from Santa Monica, in a very exclusive and expensive suburban area, from where he could see the great steely bosom of the still and endless sea long before he turned in through the wrought-iron gate of the Spence estate.

Maude Spence was finishing an early luncheon and was dressed to leave. When

153

she admitted Channing she raised a lovely eyebrow at him. He smiled. There was a kind of *rapport* between them by this time. She was still reserved, but not as icy as she'd once been. He had a theory about her, and about that: Maude Spence, badly hurt once by a man, had long since decided against any friendliness with another man. This did not mean she could not *be* friendly, it simply meant she was inhibited in that direction, unless, as with Inspector Channing, she could consider a man as something else besides a male.

It wasn't very complicated but it seemed to be, and as she led Channing on through the hall to that elegant sitting-room or reception room that showed the closed door to her dead husband's study across the entryway, he wondered if, now, a widow, no longer dependent upon a man, or *men*, with ample money for the rest of her life, she wasn't exactly where her kind of a woman ought to be: independent of everything and everyone.

But if this were so, why had she gone moonlight-riding with Doctor Linden?

As she motioned for him to be seated, Maude Spence took a nearby chair. She said, probably only making talk, that if he'd like a cup of coffee she'd have one brought in.

He declined, admired her from a distance of something like twelve feet, and said, 'You had a caller last night.'

She nodded, looking as though this was an unpleasant recollection. 'Mister Spence, Carleton's nephew. But you knew he'd be by. I told you yesterday.'

Channing had a perfect opening to mention Doctor Linden as the caller he'd been referring to, but he let it go by because he was interested in what she'd have to say about Spence. He didn't have to wait very long.

'The man is impossible, Inspector. Not only is he crude and uncouth, but he also has a dirty mind.'

Channing controlled an urge to smile. 'He has the kind of background that produces some pretty direct people, Mrs Spence.'

'Not just direct, Inspector, downright insulting. He brought up that thing about

155

my husband being physically interested in Janie Ford.'

Channing nodded. 'Anything else?'

Maude said, 'I asked him to leave. I can't imagine why he wanted to see me anyway; except to say he'd declined to contest my husband's Will — which my attorney told me this morning he wouldn't have had much luck at contesting anyway, since he and my husband were never close.'

Channing said, 'Was that your only caller?'

Instantly, the beautiful grey eyes clouded, and the handsome features settled into an expression of total impassivity. Maude cocked her head a little, reminding Channing of her former husband's attorney, who'd had the same mannerism. 'You are having me watched, Inspector? I'd have thought you wouldn't resort to things like that.'

He sidestepped confirmation or denial by saying, 'Doctor Linden?'

'Does it matter?' her anger was showing now.

Channing kept smiling at her. 'We

don't have to fence, do we? Of course it matters and you can appreciate the fact that it does. There is a murder to be resolved. Everything involving any of the people involved matters.'

She sat very primly listening to him, looking at him, then she loosened slightly. 'I'm sorry. And of course you are right. I guess my nerves are getting a little frayed.'

'That's understandable,' soothed Channing. 'To be perfectly frank, so are mine. The difference is, Mrs Spence, after this case is wrapped up, you can resume a normal life. I go right on to the next case. Frazzled nerves are a fringe benefit to my occupation.'

She smiled. 'Should I feel sorry for you, Inspector?'

'No. Just tell me what Linden wanted.'

They were back on friendly terms again, and it gave Channing a little thrill — which according to police regulations he should not have felt. Personal involvements were absolutely forbidden.

13

Engels Strikes Back

'Doctor Linden came by in response to my call to him earlier in the day. He wished to discuss business — things concerning the clinic — and after he arrived I said I would feel better if we didn't have to talk in the house. It had only been a short while earlier that my husband's nephew was there; his unpleasantness had not only permeated the house, it had also depressed me. So Doctor Linden suggested we go for a drive, seeing that it was such a lovely night.'

Maude looked expectantly at Inspector Channing when she'd finished explaining. His only question was a brief and simple one: 'Did he have supper here?'

She flushed. 'Well, not supper, no, but we did have a bit of tea and some toast, because he said he hadn't had time to eat after leaving the hospital. But when I offered to have something prepared he wouldn't hear of it. He said he'd eat later, that it wasn't very important.'

Channing kept his pleasant expression towards Mrs Spence and inwardly he called Carter Spence a highly unflattering name. The only way Spence could have thought Linden had had dinner at the Spence estate was if he'd sneaked up and peered in windows.

He most certainly couldn't have seen those people at the dining-room table from as far off as the front roadway, where he'd said he'd been waiting.

Maude said, 'Inspector, you seem bemused.'

He smiled. 'Well, I'm certainly not amused.' He straightened in the chair. 'Would you mind awfully telling me all that was discussed while you and Doctor Linden were together?'

She seemed to hesitate, but if that were so it was such a brief interlude he couldn't be certain, then she spoke. 'He is a very intense person, Inspector. I doubt if ever in his life he's ever been passive or philosophical about anything. Last night, it was overwork, personal issues, and you, that bothered him.'

'Me?'

'Well, the murder. He told me about you coming round. He also told me the full story of his affair with Janie; how Carleton had objected and all that. I told him Carleton was dead, but even if that hadn't been so, he and Janie had their own lives to lead.'

'Right enough,' approved Channing.

'As for the hospital, Inspector, it is a fact that he's overworked, but as I've told him before, I'm not the arbiter of what occurs there, Janie Ford is. He should sit down with her and together they should work out whatever seems advisable.'

Maude leaned back looking relaxed. 'There was nothing else, Inspector. He brought me home before eleven o'clock. We parted at the front door. That's all.'

Channing nodded slowly. He didn't disbelieve anything she'd said — yet. Moreover, there was a possibility that he might never disbelieve it, and unless it became pertinent to the murder, it was even more possible that he'd never bother ascertaining whether it was true or not.

He said, 'You're going out and I'm detaining you,' then rose. She didn't deny this as she also rose, but her attitude was easy, almost familiar, as she turned to walk with Channing back into the hall and down towards the front door.

'Inspector,' she said, 'if you thought Doctor Linden and I were somehow carrying on a secret love affair, believe me, apart from the fact that he's five years younger than I am, he is just too intense and — well — absorbed by other things, to have interested me years ago, let alone now.' She smiled. 'You and I are close enough to an age, Inspector, for you to know what I mean.'

He thought he knew. He also thought she was making herself out to be a good deal older than she was. He already knew her exact age, a few months shy of forty; he also was prepared at any time to swear under oath she looked ten years younger.

And there was something else. It amused him a little, but not in an uproarious way — he was five years younger than she was, so when she said they were nearly of an age it meant she thought he was about forty, and that wasn't devastating, but neither was it flattering.

After he'd left her, conscious of never having actually asked specifically what she'd meant when she'd told Linden there was nothing to worry about, that everything was going very well, he turned to speculating about Carter Spence.

He didn't see the nephew as the murderer. The man had no clear motive. At least he had none that Channing could detect. But it annoyed him having Spence making his presence larger than life with play-acting the part of a detective. It did not seem likely, though, that admonitions would produce much, because Spence wasn't a man who would be very amenable to gentle hints.

If Channing had to be damned blunt he could be, but he made a practice of avoiding that if possible. With Spence he wasn't at all sure he wouldn't fail, blunt or tactful.

Joe was entering the building from the front roadway when Channing came round the side of the building after parking his car. They saw each other and Barthelmess waited. When they met Joe raised his brows and Channing shook his head, then they entered and strode towards the stairs.

'Nothing,' murmured Channing. 'Linden feels overworked — which I think is probably true — and he's got some little personal quirks needing straightening out.'

Barthelmess said, 'Bob, that woman gets to you.'

Channing stopped, looking surprised. Joe nodded at him. It was obvious, he told the Inspector, that Maude Spence had made quite an impression upon Channing. It was also obvious, at least to Barthelmess, that her frigidity seemed several degrees less cold when she was around Channing.

Without commenting Channing walked the balance of the way to his office, and there, picking up a note one of the secretaries who took telephone calls

163

had left, he read, then mutely handed the paper to Barthelmess.

The note said simply that a man named Harding had called, had asked for Inspector Channing, and upon being told Channing was not available, had rang off without leaving a message.

'Why didn't he come see me when I was out there,' complained Channing, watching Barthelmess toss the note down. 'Have you eaten, Joe?'

'Nope. You ready?'

'Yeah.'

They left the office together. It was then slightly past two o'clock in the afternoon, which meant they wouldn't have to wait for a table at any of the local beaneries.

They didn't discuss the Spence case at all. Barthelmess, who was a great baseball fan, mentioned some high points in a recent game he'd managed to slip away and watch on television at a local tavern. Inspector Channing's personal thoughts on this were uncharitable; he did not permit himself those latitudes and didn't approve very much of other people indulging in them.

Later, as they were lighting up on the street outside the restaurant where sunshine beat down without the usual little accompanying ocean breeze, they saw Engels's attorney, Greenspan, pass in his car. They watched.

Greenspan sought a parking spot, found one, which was a minor miracle in itself, left his car, and, briefcase in hand started towards the central police department annex.

Channing said, 'Let's go. He'll have something nice for us in his magic bag.'

It was a good guess. They met the lawyer just outside Channing's office, where he'd evidently already looked in, found the room empty, and was now standing in apparent doubt as to his next move. When he saw Channing and Barthelmess appear down the corridor Greenspan's face brightened slightly. He even opened the office door and permitted them to enter first.

Channing went behind his desk while Joe took his customary chair off to one side. Their attitude was not particularly complimentary to the lawyer but Greenspan made no sign of being aware of this. He put his briefcase down as he reached to pull up a chair, and said, 'Mister Engels has instructed me to institute legal action against his former wife.' Greenspan watched for reaction. Barthelmess gazed at him, curious rather than interested. Inspector Channing sat like stone, which, if Greenspan had known him better, would have indicated just the opposite: Interest rather than curiosity.

'Go on,' said Channing. 'What grounds?'

Greenspan faltered, as though he knew what reaction his next remark would cause. He was right, for when he said, 'Breach of contract,' both detectives smiled, Joe Barthelmess's smile being broadest.

The attorney refused to recognize those expressions. He remained very businesslike although it was problematical whether he felt entirely that way. He spoke again, in a crisp tone of voice.

'Mrs Spence had an agreement with my client to make restitution for some old debts.'

'Sure,' said Joe. 'That's a lousy way for Engels to try and get himself off the hook for extortion, but it's better than not making any effort at all.'

But Channing took a different approach. 'What debts, Mister Greenspan?'

'For one, an old obligation her late husband incurred years ago.'

'Default on a personal note?' asked Channing, and shook his head before Greenspan could confirm or deny. 'Engels knows better and so do I. My guess is that you know it's a fake charge too, but even if that weren't true, as an attorney you'd also know the statues of limitations would have run out long ago.' Channing leaned. 'What's his *real* reason, Mister Greenspan; defamation, making Mrs Spence's name show up in the newspapers as being suspect? Engels may have told you his side of our extortion charge against him, but has he told you the truth?'

Greenspan made an illuminating remark. 'Inspector, I'm a lawyer. I am hired to represent people. My fee isn't large but it's large enough. I couldn't care less whether Tommy Engels comes out of this smelling like cabbage, or roses. You understand?'

Channing understood. It was the usual attitude of lawyers, and it had very little to do with what was right or wrong, legal or illegal, and it most certainly avoided contact with what was ethical or unethical; they would represent anyone and not concern themselves with a client's dishonesty, lying or blackmail, as in the case of Tommy Engels, just as long as they got paid. They didn't even mind losing the cases they took to court because any sense of defeat was assuaged by adequate compensation.

But Inspector Channing was a policemen to whom ethics mattered, odd as that was. He recoiled from the idea of Maude Spence being dragged into a courtroom and made to look bad through imputation and association. He said, 'You have some kind of trade in mind. Let's have it.'

Greenspan smiled, relieved. 'You're an astute cop. I'd heard that you were. Okay, no prosecution for my client.'

'In exchange for which there'll be no more of this talk of legal action against Mrs Spence?'

Greenspan nodded and reached to pick up his briefcase, evidently believing the visit was shortly to be completed. 'That's about it, Inspector. And since there's nothing in writing anyway, between my client and Mrs Spence, it would only be her word against Engels's word.'

'And you don't think she would be able to convince a jury?'

Greenspan shrugged. 'I don't know whether she could or not. I don't care, Inspector. My point is that she's the wife of a man who has been murdered . . . Do you see my point?'

Channing saw it. So did Joe Barthelmess. Neither of them were smiling now. Joe said casually, 'You're a slimy son of a — .'

Channing broke in, 'Never mind, Joe.' Then he said 'Mister Greenspan, you might tell your client it would be wise, at least from my point of view, for him to be very careful. You see, the police can prove he was skulking around outside the

Spence estate the night Doctor Spence was murdered. You might also explain to him that it was a *man*, not a woman, who killed Doctor Spence. Further, that since he was trying to blackmail the doctor's wife, and was the only known person sneaking around the estate that night, he's a long way from being in the clear.'

Greenspan clutched his briefcase with both hands as he listened, and after a while he inclined his head slightly as he said, 'I'll tell him, Inspector, but my advice to him will remain the same: Sue the woman to get yourself in the clear through implying doubt. It may not work, but,' Greenspan rose, faintly smiling, 'but as I've said before, I'm only a lawyer trying to serve a client, and I get paid no matter who else loses.'

Inspector Channing nodded and didn't arise. 'You'd better give your client some good advice, Mister Greenspan, because what you've just tried to do here amounts to blackmail again — *legal* blackmail, perhaps, but whether the

District Attorney will take that view or not I can't say. If he doesn't, you may find things a little hot for you, personally, before the local Bar Association. Goodbye, Mister Greenspan.'

14

Emergency!

Inspector Channing was curious about what it was John Harding wanted to see him about, but the next day being Sunday, he drove up-country to the burnt-over Malibu Hills where, south of Point Hueneme, there was a smelly boat-dock and a number of small, sturdy fishing boats for charter.

He went alone, as he usually did, and fished out beyond the breakers some fifteen miles. The skipper was an old friend. Perhaps Joe Barthelmess liked baseball but Channing liked participation-sports. He'd been chartering the same boat for several years. He and the captain, a weathered, gravel-voiced person named Carl Johnson, were old friends.

But the fishing was poor. Captain Johnson swore up and down there were Russian trawlers off the coast and that they slipped inside the twelve-mile-limit after nightfall and seined back and forth only a few miles offshore, which resulted in a great dearth of fish.

Channing didn't really care very much. He liked the battle the fish put up, especially the large ones, but it was the pitch of the sturdy little ugly boat, the sound and scent of the sea, the cry of gulls overhead, and the sense of being detached from everything that otherwise cluttered his life, that was so pleasant.

Captain Johnson had cheese and biscuits, sardines and beer for their lunch. The grey haze that monotonously hung over the land, thickening as it reached farther inland towards Los Angeles proper, rose like a soiled wall from the nearest land. Captain Johnson said he'd been watching the encroachment of that smog for years, having long since promised himself if and when it reached as far north as his rickety boat-dock, he would up-anchor and head for the Oregon coast where a man might still draw a fresh breath of air.

The day passed pleasantly. Later, in the early dusk when Inspector Channing reached his flat, feeling sticky from salt-spray, tired and uncomplicated, the telephone rang. It was Joe Barthelmess. He had been reached by Maude Spence when she'd been unable to reach Channing.

'She was a little upset,' said Joe, 'but between you and me I can't share her feelings.'

'Okay. What's happened?'

'Ford had another heart-seizure. His daughter telephoned Mrs Spence. She tried to reach you.'

Channing was baffled. 'Why me? I'm no doctor.'

'I know. I didn't ask her why. Anyway, she said Janie had had her father taken to the clinic, so I guess there's no point in either of us getting in a stew. We'll be on it tomorrow anyway.'

Channing agreed, rang off, went to take a shower, and afterwards dressed in a suit instead of sports shirt and slacks, went down to his car and drove out to the clinic. He wasn't happy, but he also wouldn't have been happy if he'd sat around watching television, either.

Janie was in Doctor Linden's office

with a tear-streaked face. She blinked up at Channing as though he were some kindly member of the family, letting words tumble forth about the terrible shock it had been to find her father out in his back garden trying to catch his breath and stand up after he'd crumpled to the grass.

Channing could appreciate what an experience it must have been. He patted her shoulder and asked if Doctor Linden was attending her father.

'Yes,' she wavered. 'But I wish Doctor Spence were here. He was so experienced in cases like this.'

Channing went to the window of Linden's office and saw that the lovely tree-shaded yard beyond was empty of convalescents. He lit a cigarette, turned and studied Janie. She was making a successful and gallant attempt to control her emotions.

Channing said, 'What did he say, when you found him?'

Her answer was short. 'Nothing. What could he say, he couldn't even breathe and the pain was terrible. His face was white and terribly twisted from suffering.'

Channing wondered if it had been the heart, or the pacemaker wired to pectoral muscles, that had failed. Instead of making direct enquiry he asked if Doctor Linden had told her anything yet.

He'd only said he had her father under an oxygen tent and that he'd undertaken to make certain through the use of larger, more dependable pulsating equipment, that the heart's labours would be minimized in order that it might rest.

'Was he hopeful, Janie?'

She nodded without looking very encouraged. 'Yes. But he's sent for a specialist. I think he just doesn't want me to worry.'

'Why did you call Mrs Spence?' he asked, and her reaction was almost instantaneous — and hostile.

'Are you *always* a policeman? Doesn't it matter to you that my father may be dying?'

He took the rebuke as he took all rebukes of this kind, without showing corresponding irritation. 'It matters, Janie.

If there was anything at all I could do, I'd do it. But you're correct, I am always a policeman. If I weren't — if thousands of other Los Angeles detectives weren't always policemen — believe me, you'd have a lot less to be thankful for right now.'

The reproach was delivered mildly and Channing afterwards gently smiled into the girl's upturned, troubled face. 'Why Mrs Spence?' he asked again.

She answered tonelessly, 'I don't know. She's the first person I thought of.'

Channing stood gazing downward. The *first* person? Aside from the obviousness of William Linden being a physician, if she loved him wouldn't she have thought of him first? Then she spoke on, and Channing's question was answered.

'I knew Will wouldn't be at the clinic yet. He and I went surfing earlier and when he left me at my house, before I found my father out in the back garden, Will said he had to take his car to some special place for work to be done on it. The motor, he said, was getting rough. It sounded fine to me, but then I know nothing about cars and Will does.'

'But you finally reached him?'

Janie shook her head. 'No, I had my father brought here, and Will was just arriving. He didn't intend to stay, just look in. After all, this is Sunday.'

'You were very fortunate,' said Channing, and turned back to gazing out the window until several minutes later when Doctor Linden entered the office looking more baffled than anxious. Janie sprang up and ran into his arms. He saw Channing and looked surprised.

'You knew?' asked Linden.

Channing explained about Mrs Spence's call to Joe Barthelmess and his own involvement through Joe. He put out his cigarette and waited for Janie to be calmed by the physician.

Linden, disengaging himself, said, 'Look, love, your father will probably be all right. The specialist will be here shortly. Now I want you to go down the hall to the sunroom and relax. Read a magazine down there, or watch television, but relax. As soon as the specialist has had his say, I'll come let you know how things stand.

Will you do that, please?'

Janie nodded and left the office.

Linden sank down into a chair and said, 'Hell of a thing, Inspector.'

'Why is it? People who have bad hearts usually relapse don't they?'

'Sooner or later, only I don't quite understand this one. The pacemaker malfunctioned, and yet when I had a look at it a moment ago, after making sure Ford would hang on under the tent and with the other equipment taking over, I couldn't find anything wrong with the thing.' Linden looked up. 'But I'm no great shakes with those things. I'll have to get a trained man in on it tomorrow.'

The intercom on Linden's desk buzzed and he went to answer it. The specialist had arrived and was waiting at the reception desk. Linden told Channing he'd be back after a bit and left the room.

For a while Inspector Channing remained over by the window, then he stepped to the desk, hoisted the telephone and called Joe Barthelmess.

His request was simple and direct.

'Joe, contact someone at the lab who knows electronics, explain where this clinic is and tell him I want someone to come right out here and examine one of those pacemaker heart pumps. Be sure you get someone who will know what he's doing.'

After Channing rang off he ambled on down the hall in search of the sunroom. When he found Janie Ford she was doing neither of the things Doctor Linden had asked, but was standing in front of a window beyond which were visible the city lights of Santa Monica, far southward, and in the opposite direction, the great glow against the sky that night-time Los Angeles made.

She turned when he entered. He could see that she'd been crying again, so the questions in his mind remained there, and instead, he said, 'The specialist is here. I think between the two doctors they'll make as sure as possible your father recovers.'

Janie had evidently been having some unemotional thoughts. She said, 'Doctor

Spence told me those electronic pumps didn't fail.'

Channing knew better. Anything mechanical, just like anything made of flesh and bone, eventually failed. 'It was fortunate for him you came along when you did. When he recovers he'll owe you something.'

'*If* he recovers, Inspector.'

Channing wasn't going to step into that trap. He said, 'Everything will be done, Janie, that can be done.' He picked up a magazine. It dealt with the world of women so he put it back down again. 'Has that pacemaker ever acted up before?'

She turned to look at him, shaking her head. 'My father said it was genuine miracle; that he'd never felt as safe and healthy in his life, since Doctor Spence installed it. Before that, he'd have those chest pains. The medicine worked for a while but he didn't have much confidence in it. He once asked me what would happen if he suffered an attack in his sleep? The pacemaker worked round the clock. It made him feel perfectly secure. Then — this!'

Channing had pursued this subject as far as he cared to. He spoke of other things, of her father's health in general, and once, when Janie gave him the opening by saying that since her mother's death her father had seemed to lose interest in life, he asked if she remembered her mother, not because he was interested but because it gave him a chance to divert her thoughts from the current dilemma.

'I remember her very well. I was a child when she died, but not a small one at all. She was very sweet and understanding. We used to go on picnics up the coast when she was alive. My father was devoted to her. After she died — well — he had trouble for a long time just hanging on. I suppose I recovered from the loss more quickly, being younger.'

A car's headlamps came up the curving driveway. They both turned to watch that, then Channing excused himself. He had recognized the vehicle as being one of those unmarked departmental sedans.

Joe Barthelmess was with the laboratory

technician. Channing was surprised about that and Joe grinned as he said, 'Couldn't keep my mind on television after I called you. What's up?'

Channing shook hands with the lab man, an individual named Fogarty, and related all that he knew. Then he led the two men inside and along the silent corridor to Linden's office. There, they discussed what had brought them together, until Doctor Linden returned.

Fogarty knew pacemakers; he explained how they worked, what motivated them, and how they could co-ordinate the heart's functions. He also described what possibly could cause one to fail but his personal opinion was that if Frank Ford had taken care of the device — and he couldn't imagine a person whose life depended on such a device not taking care of it — there actually was little reason for a malfunction.

'Of course it could happen. Anything is possible, in that respect. But if Ford had taken all the precautions, barring something faulty in the construction itself, I'd be inclined to wonder what happened.'

'Something was faulty in the construction, as you say,' suggested Barthelmess, and Fogarty looked at him.

'If that thing had been operating for any length of time, Joe, and had been faulty at the beginning, believe me it would have failed long before this.'

That remark left both Barthelmess and Channing staring at the laboratory technician.

15

Channing has a Hunch

When Doctor Linden finally reached his office and was introduced to Fogarty, it was close to midnight and he looked drawn out.

He said the specialist was still with Mister Ford, and that he'd just come from seeing Janie. He had told her to go on home, that her father was responding very well; that in fact if his recovery continued as well as it seemed now to be doing, she'd be able to visit him the next evening.

Channing was pleased. 'What do you suppose could have caused the trouble?' he asked. 'Do you suppose Mister Fogarty could see the pacemaker, Doctor?'

Linden looked briefly annoyed, which was understandable; he had just come through a very trying period after a trying day. But he curbed his impatience and nodded. 'Come with me, Mister Fogarty,' he said, and left the room.

When Joe and Channing were alone, Barthelmess said, 'What's on your mind, Bob?'

Channing shook his head. 'Nothing. Well, that's not exactly true. But nothing I can put a finger on, Joe. Ford's artificial heart let him down. It's a reasonable happening.'

'But you're wondering why?'

'Yes. Everyone, including Doctor Spence, said those things were very reliable; that with care they didn't malfunction. But this one did.'

Barthelmess was unimpressed. 'What of it? I mean, supposing it *wasn't* a logical malfunction?'

'That's the thing that's bothering me,' answered Channing. 'Ford was a small frog in a big pool. No one paid any attention to him and he was outside the mainstream of everything that's happened . . . Or was he, Joe? Maybe we've been blinded by the forest until we couldn't see one particular tree.'

Barthelmess looked aside and hid a

yawn. 'One objection to your sinister suspicions, Bob. The Coroner's report said a guy with a lot of muscle rammed that knife into Doctor Spence. I've only seen this Ford a couple of times but even with padded shoulders I can tell you that stripped down he'd look like the ninety-seven pound weakling in those advertisements for liver extract. He couldn't even swat a fly hard, let alone shove a big knife into someone's chest.'

Channing didn't dispute this, but he said, 'I'm not claiming Frank Ford killed Spence, Joe. I'm simply wondering what might lie behind the failure of the man's heart-machine — if the thing was in good shape.'

Barthelmess looked at his wrist. 'How long will it take Fogarty with that device, I wonder?'

Channing made no reply because he had no answer. He knew only what he'd read about pacemakers, and hadn't retained very much of that.

It was well he hadn't tried to make a guess because an hour later Fogarty returned looking puzzled. 'I've got to take this thing down to the lab,' he said. 'There's no testing or analysing equipment here.'

Channing said he'd clear this with Doctor Linden. He then said, 'From what you've seen so far, what does it look like?'

Fogarty's answer was terse. 'That's the problem, Inspector. Right now, it doesn't look to me like there was anything wrong with the damned thing.'

That was all Fogarty would commit himself to although both the detectives tried to get him to be more explicit. In the end, Barthelmess went with Fogarty, and they both left Inspector Channing alone at the clinic. It was then almost two o'clock in the morning and Channing's eyelids felt as though they had specks of grit beneath them.

When Doctor Linden finally returned to sag into a chair at his desk, he said the specialist was gone. He also said, gazing from red eyes at Channing, 'That gentleman's bill will be something for you to digest, Inspector, feeling as you do about physicians and their charges. You can't get a man of that one's stature in the middle of the night without it costing a lot of money.' Channing would concede this, since he didn't really feel very concerned. He explained about authorizing the police technician's removal of the pacemaker to the departmental laboratory, and although he expected some indignation, there was none. Probably because Doctor Linden was too tired to protest.

He merely said, 'If your man doesn't know what he's doing, Inspector, he can ruin the chances of an experienced man looking at the thing.'

Channing could reassure Linden on that score, and did so. He then said he'd like to know what the specialist thought.

Linden obliged but without enthusiasm. 'Nothing I hadn't already concluded, Inspector. Ford's artificial aid malfunctioned and the resultant shock to his heart was a bit much. Frankly, the man's damned lucky to be alive. He's also damned lucky I happened along when I did for otherwise there would have been no one here to help him, and he couldn't have hung on very long without something being done. But there is one thing in Ford's favour; he doesn't exert. I've known him ever since I've known his daughter and I've yet to see him get perturbed about anything, or even take much of an interest in anything. Handling Doctor Spence's buildings isn't difficult work; the tenants are substantial people. Once a month Ford goes round collecting. As a matter of fact, as I've said to Janie, her father's present position was made to order for a man in his shape.'

All this interested Channing, but not very much. He said, 'Did you know Janie had called Mrs Spence?'

Linden nodded. 'She told me. What of it?'

'I was wondering if Mrs Spence had called you, Doctor?'

The answer was a mild surprise to Channing. Linden said, 'Yes, as a matter of fact she did call. But I couldn't spare her very much time at the moment. I was getting Ford set up for the oxygen, you see.'

'What did she say, Doctor?'

'That she would pay for the specialist, when I told her I had called for one. That's all, Inspector. I rang off.'

Channing rose, hid a yawn and smiled. 'I'm partial to these nice, quiet Sundays, Doctor. Good night.'

He left Doctor Linden sitting behind his desk looking disconsolate, and in fact Channing didn't feel very different himself. It was one of the quirks of his nature that Channing never rested well as long as there was a riddle bothering him.

But he slept for several hours after getting back to his flat, and when Joe Barthelmess came dragging in the next morning, Channing was already at his desk looking shaved and coffee-ed.

Joe asked if Fogarty had called. He hadn't, Channing could report, for the most excellent reason that he'd invoked an old regulation that allowed overworked personnel to take a corresponding amount of time off the next day.

Barthelmess groaned. 'If I'd known I'd

have done it too. Now where are we?'

'Nowhere,' confessed Channing. 'Linden says Ford is better this morning. I called a bit ago.'

'That's all?'

'No. Janie called me. She wanted to apologize for being out-of-sorts last night.'

'Was she?'

Channing nodded. 'With every good reason a person could have. Especially a person with only one parent left. And there's one other thing — probably unimportant — but Mrs Spence volunteered to pay for that heart specialist.'

Barthelmess, still adhering to his strong suspicion of Maude Spence, perked up a little. 'Maybe she was having an — '

Channing raised a warning hand. 'Joe, you're not awake yet. You said last night Frank Ford was too puny to ram a knife into Spence, so how could he be strong enough to be having an affair with a beautiful and very healthy widow?'

Barthelmess slumped, fished for his smokes and lit one. It apparently didn't taste very good because halfway through he punched it out in Channing's desk ashtray.

A little later, when they were preparing to go out to luncheon, Fogarty called from the laboratory. Channing said they'd stop by the lab on the way back from lunch and Fogarty had a better idea; he would meet them out front and go to lunch with them.

When they saw him, Fogarty looked fit and smiling. He was perhaps one of those people who didn't require as much rest as other mortals. Or else, having arrived late, he'd got all the rest he'd been cheated out of the night before.

As the three of them headed towards a cross-walk keeping wary eyes on the snarling lanes of traffic, Fogarty suggested a Hungarian restaurant. Neither Channing nor Barthelmess objected, so Fogarty led the way.

It was a pleasant place, slightly off the beaten path and therefore not very crowded. It was also gloomy enough inside, with its subdued lighting and dark walls, to be cool.

They got a rear table, ordered, then

Fogarty said, 'I had a man look at that damned pacemaker who used to make those things for an electronics outfit. There was nothing wrong with it.'

Joe swore. 'Of course there was. Or do you mean Ford's heart acted up in spite of the device?'

'That's possible,' said Fogarty. 'Doctor Linden or some other medic could give you that answer, but I'll tell you this: if I needed one of those things I'd be perfectly willing to use that one. It's as sound as the day it was fitted to Ford.'

That bit of information stumped Channing completely. He ate his lunch in almost sullen silence, and afterwards he only asked one question of Fogarty.

'Suppose a man wearing that thing had fallen. Suppose that somehow he'd got it unhooked.'

Fogarty's answer was quick and convincing. 'Those things are attached to take any shock that a human body would normally encounter. You could fall with the thing and unless you fell hard enough to crush it — which would also crush you, believe me — it wouldn't be hurt.'

They were walking back to the building again, with hot midday sunlight beating down upon them. The stench of exhaust fumes from traffic plus the wicked glare of lemon-yellow brilliance made their eyes sting. Joe used a handkerchief before they reached the building and Fogarty set up a stiffer pace. But Channing plodded along as though barely conscious of the smog, the perilous traffic, the constant and endless rumble of the city that surrounded them.

When they parted, Fogarty heading for the cool cleanliness of his laboratory, Channing and Barthelmess heading for the office, Channing finally spoke.

'It's got a bad odour, Joe.'

Barthelmess wasn't convinced. 'Look, maybe the thing didn't go sour. But you heard what Fogarty said. Ford's heart could have acted up.'

Channing already had figured out the answer to that. Doctor Linden had told him the night before, and again this morning, that Frank Ford's heart was recovering very well.

'A man,' he told Joe, as they shuffled

back into the little office, 'whose heart almost stops, doesn't make any speedy recovery, Joe. Linden told me last night it was almost miraculous the way Ford was recovering. This morning he told me the same thing again. While I was waiting for you to show up this morning, I telephoned one of the department physicians. He said that very often hearts make a great initial recovery — then stop.'

Barthelmess looked quizzical. 'You're arguing against your own argument, Bob.'

'No. The doctor said a man in Ford's condition might have made great strides last night, under oxygen and with other stimulants, but by this morning when the treatment was being allowed to slacken off so the heart could make its own adjustment, that was when it would simply stop beating.'

'I see. And Linden told you everything was going along gung-ho?'

'Yes.'

Barthelmess kept gazing at Inspector Channing. 'So now you've got something else you're hung up on. What is it?'

'I had in mind a very unauthorized job of breaking and entering.'

Barthelmess blinked. 'Where — the Spence place?'

'No. The Ford cottage. You care to violate regulations as my guest, or would you prefer to remain in this air-conditioned building counting up the years you still have to serve before you can retire on a full pension — without any risk of getting sacked?'

Barthelmess grinned, 'I like risk. Would you believe that's why I became a policeman, lo, those many years ago?'

Channing headed for the door and Joe Barthelmess followed after him.

16

A Latent Clue

It was on the drive to Sixteenth Street that Joe Barthelmess said, 'Bob, I don't get the connection between going out here and looking in the Ford cottage, and Ford's heart attack.'

Channing's answer wasn't very enlightening. 'There may not be a connection, Joe.'

'You sure as hell aren't going into this house without some idea that it could be necessary.'

Channing turned off the throughway on to Sixteenth Street before saying, 'Something is wrong, Joe. I don't pretend to know what it is, but my hunch is that there may be an answer out here.'

'We didn't have to make an unauthorized entry. Janie'd have okayed a search,' said Barthelmess, as they crossed several intersecting residential roads before slowing to a halt out front of the Ford cottage.

Channing didn't dispute this at all. In fact, he didn't comment on it. He got out of the car and headed for the rear yard where Ford's garden was, and where Janie had said she'd found him.

Barthelmess followed. He also made a careful study of his surroundings; unlike Inspector Channing who had been here before, Joe Barthelmess's familiarity included the entire neighbourhood rather than any one particular house in it.

The garden was about as Channing remembered it; well-tended, attractive, and fragrant. The grass had been clipped recently and a Chinese Elm tree in a corner of the garden had been pruned.

The cottage itself occupied the front two-thirds of the bit of land it sat upon, and there was an attached two-car garage, one half of which had long ago been converted into some kind of storage shed or workshop, Channing didn't know which because the door was locked.

The car in the other half of the garage hadn't been new in quite a few years, and as Joe pointed out, according to the light

199

skiff of dust upon it and underneath it, the car probably hadn't been driven in a long while as well.

The house was open, which at first made Channing believe Janie might be home, but she wasn't. As Joe said, if she'd been home she would doubtless have come to see what they were doing in the rear garden. He also said something else: 'If she went off leaving the house unlocked, she's probably at the neighbourhood market and will return any minute.'

Channing wasn't very concerned, evidently, because he began a systematic examination of the interior of the house.

There were two bedrooms, both at the back of the house, along with a small dining alcove between parlour and kitchen, plus a rear porch which doubled as coat-room and laundry. Two baths, each one off one of the bedrooms, completed the house.

It was not a new residence and seemed to have been built with a view of frugality guiding its builder. It was solid enough, and probably comfortable, but it had no excess space at all, and in the interests of economy where the bedrooms might easily have been twelve by fifteen feet, they were instead twelve by thirteen feet.

In the bedroom they felt certain belonged to Frank Ford there was an oxygen bottle in a corner, possibly for instant use if he suffered chest pains while abed, and the furniture was almost Spartan in its severity and also in its functional utility; there was a dresser with a mirror, a bed, one chair, one bedstand with a reading lamp.

Barthelmess shook his head. 'I'd get gloomy just having to sleep in here.'

The other bedroom was light, airy, and an artistic hand had wrought magic at the curtained windows, at the colour combinations between walls and ceiling, even with the drab furniture which had been re-worked until it looked downright cheery.

There was also a bookcase, half-filled with what seemed to be University texts, a solitary slalom ski, two spear guns for use with the scuba skin-diving suit lying across a chair, and a number of feminine adornments that drew no interest from either of the detectives.

When they went to the kitchen, then on through the little dining alcove into the sitting-room, Joe Barthelmess was beginning to look a little sceptical. He had every right, Channing hadn't said that he was looking for anything in particular, and as far as Barthelmess could see, this was just another little cottage, humbly furnished, pleasantly located, and with nothing to redeem it from the category of sameness it shared with perhaps a million similar places within a radius of ten miles.

Channing finally led the way back outside, offered Barthelmess a smoke from his packet, lit up for them both then said, 'Well, pretty commonplace, I'd call it.'

Joe was sardonic. 'This is what I risked my neck for — unauthorized entry into a little house as drab as dozens just like it I've seen in my lifetime, and for nothing more dramatic than just that one fact?'

Channing grinned. 'I promised nothing,

Joe. If you'll remember you asked to come along.'

'I'm not griping, Bob, but I'm bewildered. What did you expect to find out here?'

'I don't know. Nothing, possibly. But this is the one area we've neglected in the Spence affair.'

Barthelmess wasn't enthusiastic. 'Okay, and now we've covered it. And I'm hungry, so how about heading back and grabbing a corned-beef on rye at the first clean-looking restaurant.'

Channing led the way to the car but when they were circling the square to reach the throughway, he said, 'We'll get something to eat if you like, Joe, but I want to stop by the clinic on the way back and see how Frank Ford's doing.'

That is exactly what they did, but Doctor Linden was giving an examination to a new admittee so they were taken to the waiting room by an attractive red-headed nurse, and left there.

Channing made conversation by explaining this was what was also called the sunroom, and that it was here he and

Janie Ford'd had their last little visit the night of her father's admittance to the clinic. Barthelmess was bored.

Linden came along after a bit looking fresh and rested, looking almost cheerful as they all shook hands and Linden asked if they wouldn't prefer going on up to his private office. Channing vetoed that on the grounds that they hadn't stopped by for any actual discussion, they were just in the area and had wondered about Frank Ford.

Doctor Linden spread his hands. 'Remarkable recovery, gentlemen. I had the specialist back again to verify my own enthusiasm because it just seemed unreasonable, or at the very least highly unusual, for a heart patient to respond so well.'

Channing was pleased and smiled. 'And when you send him home, Doctor . . . ?'

'Well, of course he'll be fitted with a new pacemaker. Not by me, of course, I'm not qualified in the speciality, but by others who are. And of course for several weeks he can do little more than shave himself and feed himself; in other words, he'll have to return to his former state very, very gradually, and there is the possibility that he won't be able to come up to the former condition at all, depending upon what additional damage his heart may have suffered in this most recent seizure.'

Channing listened and nodded, and asked when he might see Mister Ford. To this request Doctor Linden looked slightly surprised, as though a sudden thought had just come to him.

'Why, Inspector, I suppose you could see him tomorrow or the next day. But I'm sure he won't be able to tell you anything except that his heart acted up.'

Channing thanked Doctor Linden and departed with Joe Barthelmess trailing along. On their continued drive to police headquarters Joe said, 'You think someone tried to kill Ford, don't you?'

Channing was careful when he answered. 'How does it look to you? It wasn't the pacemaker. Fogarty says that is definite.'

'Hell,' exclaimed Barthelmess, 'all that means is that Ford's heart cut up. You surely can't believe someone influenced that to happen.'

'It's possible, Joe, simply by tampering with the pacemaker upon which Ford's heart depended for its pulsation promptings. If someone interfered with the continuity of those pulsations Ford's heart, which was quite weak without those assists, would act up.'

Barthelmess turned this over in his mind and finally, shortly before they were heading into the parking area at police headquarters, he said, 'Do you know what you are probably saying, Bob? You're accusing Janie Ford of plotting to kill her own father.'

'Not necessarily, Janie. In fact, she has the best alibi. She was out surfing with Doctor Linden.'

'Tell me this,' said Barthelmess as they trudged towards a side door into the building, 'how did this ectoplasmic suspect of yours slip up on Ford while he was working in his garden, unseen and unheard, and foul up Ford's heart? Bob, you're reaching too far out this time.'

Channing's answer was unperturbed.

'Maybe I'm reaching out too far, but I'll tell you one thing, Joe, *something* happened in Frank Ford's back garden, and it came within an ace of killing him. That is fact number one. Fact number two is that there is some kind of damned discrepancy in all this that I can't quite identify yet, but which exists.'

'The identity of a murderer,' said Barthelmess, hiking up the stairs beside Channing. 'Suppose we verify the whereabouts of everyone involved in the Spence murder, for that period of time when Ford had his heart attack.'

Channing was perfectly agreeable, but as soon as they reached the office there was an interruption. Another note left by one of the women who took telephone calls, said that John Harding had telephoned Inspector Channing again.

Barthelmess shrugged. 'Go and see him. 'I'll do that other little job of checking everyone out. If Harding has anything worthwhile to add to what we already know, I'll be waiting to hear it when you get back this evening.'

Inspector Channing had no aversion

to practically retracing his earlier steps in order to reach the Spence estate. He had been coming to look forward with some pleasure to each visit out there for some time now.

But of course his timing, undoubtedly because he invariably arrived unannounced and unexpected, could not always be as good as he might have wished. On this visit it wasn't. Maude Spence had left for the city an hour earlier, according to the maid.

Channing hadn't come to see her anyway. He went ambling round the grounds in search of the yardman, and found him eventually in a delightfully cool and shady place where a number of exotic tropical flowers grew, mostly gorse-like, hugging the ground and spreading out, but also standing like tall bushes, their leaves star-drop shaped, their flowers large and speckled, and scented with the slightly overpowering mimosa scent one usually found in tropical gardens.

Harding was as brown as a berry and when he smiled his teeth were a startling white. He offered to take

Inspector Channing round to his quarters but Channing pointed to a stone bench nearby in the shade of a clutch of birch trees, and Harding went over there with him.

Channing didn't push. Harding was a nervous man, easily upset; in time he'd get round to whatever it was that had prompted him to telephone Channing.

Harding didn't smoke, so when Channing lit up it gave the gardener a bit more time to get organized. Finally, the yardman said, 'That night of Doctor Spence's killing . . . '

'Yes?'

'Well, that day and the day before I'd been preparing a seed bed for some rhododendrons, you see, and the day after the murder I found several imprints of a man's shoe in the freshly mulched soil.'

'You've been a bit long getting round to telling me, Harding.'

'I had no reason to believe they didn't belong to the doctor himself, Inspector, or to one of those men, yourself included, who came swarming over the place afterwards.'

'How do you know they didn't belong to some of those men?'

'Inspector, I've been at it two weeks now, but I can show you a set of your footprints, the prints of Mister Barthelmess, Mister Ford, Mister Carter Spence, and several others. I've been collecting them very carefully since the morning of the murder, you see, and not a one of them fits the imprints I've preserved of that unknown man who walked across the rhododendron bed. If you'll come along to my quarters, Inspector, I'll show you what I mean.'

Harding rose. Channing gazed up at the man with an expression of almost resignation. Oh Lord, another amateur sleuth, and this one, God bless him, had been concealing evidence — namely, footprints of a probable murderer!

17

An Assist from John Harding

Harding had not exaggerated. He showed Channing several neatly arranged mud imprints, hardened to a brittle consistency and carefully brought to a flowerbed near the south end of the garage-annexe where Harding lived.

Each set of prints had been labelled — not necessarily with accuracy; Channing's name had been spelt with only one n — but with integrity. Harding invited Channing to remove his shoe and place it gently within the preserved imprint with his name upon it. Channing chose not to avail himself of this sterling opportunity, although he knelt with Harding gazing at the footprints.

They were all there, even one allegedly belonging to Doctor Linden. Harding explained that it had taken a great deal of patience to make this accumulation and

211

Channing, finally satisfied the impressions were genuine, began making comparisons between them. He had, for example, never before noticed that Joe Barthelmess had such *broad* feet, long ones, yes, but uncommonly broad as well.

He could very easily verify his own imprints, and when Harding offered to show that the impressions he'd made of his feet were true, Channing gazed at the man.

'How did you happen to do this? I mean, those imprints from the flowerbed you feel were left by the murderer notwithstanding, I get the impression you were familiar with what you were doing — taking imprints.'

Harding lifted the set of unidentified footprints and set them very gently before Channing as he answered. 'In Korea I was part of a mine-laying team. We perfected the study of tracks in order to know which trails and roads were most likely to be travelled so we could mine them. It got to be a sort of game among us — studying feet, tracks, the imprints people made. Sometimes it was possible to tell a good deal about a man by his imprints.'

Channing straightened up gazing at those impressions Harding had placed in front of him. He didn't mention the matter of withholding evidence. Not yet anyway, but he said, 'From your experience, then, Mister Harding, what would you deduce from these unidentified imprints?'

Harding was ready for that enquiry. 'The man was fair-sized — his feet are longer. But he probably did not weigh more than average for his height — the impressions are not deep despite the fact he crossed fresh-turned earth. From length of stride it seems he might have been wanting to move off fast, but without making a lot of noise or drawing attention to himself. And Inspector, there's one other thing; the direction these tracks was taking across the flowerbed was away from the front gate, towards a heavy thicket of hedge farther to the left. Now that puzzles me.'

It puzzled Channing too, until he

strolled round the edge of the annexe to stand a moment gazing down towards the wrought-iron gate, then it no longer puzzled him.

He did not mention it to Harding, but the night of the murder Maude Spence had hastened towards the yonder roadway to meet Engels, and she'd indicated to Channing that Engels, after flashing his lights, had driven southward, which would be to the left of the gate.

The unidentified man had gone northward, which would be to the right of the gate. Channing's conclusion was that although Mrs Spence had said she hadn't seen anyone, someone had seen her, and had gone off in the opposite direction to avoid detection.

Fair enough, but when Channing asked Harding who he thought those imprints might belong to, he drew a total blank. Harding didn't know. In fact, he said he'd been studying every recent track each day since the murder and had not found any more tracks like those he felt belonged to the murderer. He offered the imprints to Channing. They returned to Harding's quarters, found an adequate cardboard box, wrapped each little bit of indented mud very carefully in newspaper, then Channing took the box to the car, with Harding hiking along beside him. And Channing still did not mention the withholding of evidence. In fact, he never did mention it to Harding, although when he was back at his office showing the imprints to Joe Barthelmess, he said something about it, rather profanely too.

Barthelmess grinned. 'Cops are always griping about lack of citizen co-operation. You ought to be grateful.'

They took the impressions down to the laboratory and left them, not expecting any spectacular revelations, which was fortunate, then they went out for mid-afternoon coffee and a general discussion which posed more questions by far than it provided answers to.

Later, shortly before it was time to quit for the day, Fogarty telephoned from the laboratory to report that the mud showed indications of having been taken from a freshly spaded plot of earth, which

Channing already knew, and to also report that the man who made those imprints seemed to be stretching his stride to its maximum length, which Channing also knew. The only information the lab man had to impart that Channing had occasion to reflect upon, was the fact that the man who made those impressions wore shoes which, although far from new, showed actually no trace of hard usage at all.

Barthelmess, when informed of this latter revelation, looked annoyed. 'That makes sense like a hole in the head. How can you wear an old pair of shoes and not have them show wear?'

Upon that riddle Joe decided to call it a day, but after he'd departed Inspector Channing sat for a long while gently rocking forth and back in his squeaky old desk-chair, and finally he telephoned Maude Spence to ascertain that she would receive him that evening.

She agreed, but she sounded slightly amused when she reiterated an implication she'd previously made, to the effect that Channing never seemed to sleep.

He had dinner on the way out, bought a fresh packet of cigarettes, then took his time reaching the estate. There was still considerable daylight left when he drove through the gate, but then the days were beginning to lengthen as springtime gave way to summer. Also, the days were getting steadily warmer while the evenings became more predictably pleasant.

There was the sliver of a scimitar-moon overhead, and far out where mingling daylight and nightlight lay across the heaving sea, there was a timelessness that was restful to the eyes as well as the spirit.

Maude Spence met Channing out in front. She was dressed for comfort, from which he deduced her stay in the city throughout most of the earlier day hadn't been pleasant, probably due to the smog, the humid heat, and the nerve-wracking noise of Los Angeles.

She offered to take him indoors but he preferred the fragrant grounds and said so. She smiled in composed agreement, and after studying him a moment she said, 'You have a problem, Inspector.'

He looked at her with a twinkle. 'I always have at least one problem, and usually it's a dozen, one on top of another. This time I can tell you that although you did not see your husband's murderer, he saw you.'

She stopped smiling. 'That — night . . . ?'

'Yes. I'm sure that the pair of you either passed one another, or else that he was already at the house when you went down towards the road, and that after he'd been inside and emerged again, he cautiously took a direction that would preclude an inadvertent meeting.'

'Is there a significance, Inspector?'

'Probably. There are also footprints, Mrs Spence, of a tallish, lean man with a lengthy stride.'

She seemed to consider those qualifications for a moment. Eventually she said, 'Harding? He's tall and lean.' She suddenly raised a hand to her lips.

Channing stood gazing at her. He knew what had suddenly crossed her mind because he'd had the same thought earlier.

She half whispered a name. 'Tommy Engels . . . ?'

Channing was matter-of-fact. 'Yes, the description would also fit him.'

Then she made a little gesture of bewilderment. 'But it would also fit Will Linden, wouldn't it?'

'Possibly,' he conceded. 'But I believe we can eliminate Harding.' He didn't give her his reasons for this.

'Inspector, that description would fit you. It would fit a dozen of my husband's acquaintance that I can think of.'

Channing offered no rebuttal although he felt his own size, while compatible, was offset by his weight, which was near enough two hundred pounds to negate the possibility of anyone considering him lean.

Maude looked down towards the soft-lighted front gate, a fair distance from where she stood, and Channing thought he detected a slight shudder. She said, 'He could have killed me too.'

'They don't usually, Mrs Spence. I mean, murderers — excepting the rare mad ones — do not run amok and kill people arbitrarily. Your husband's killer had his mind set on just one victim. It's even possible that if he'd thought you'd seen him before he reached the house, he would have fled without even trying to reach the house.'

She raised grey, thoughtful eyes. 'Why couldn't it have worked out that way?'

Channing had no answer to that, but he had an alternate suggestion. 'The man who killed your husband, Mrs Spence, knew exactly what he intended to do. If he had been frightened off that night, he'd have come back.'

She accepted that, evidently, because she moved on to something else. 'Inspector, when will it end?'

He said, 'Very shortly now.'

She gazed at him in some surprise. He'd sounded so confident. 'You know who the murderer is . . . ?'

He smiled gently. 'I have a pretty good idea, Mrs Spence.'

'I see . . . But you wouldn't be willing to say?'

'No.'

She stood a moment considering him,

then she said, 'Would you like some coffee — or perhaps a highball?' The words had scarcely left her then she quickly said, 'I'm sorry. I'll cancel the highball. I heard somewhere you aren't allowed to drink on duty. Well, how about the coffee?'

Channing would have liked that very much, but he declined. He didn't explain why, not to her, but to himself it was very elemental. He had said, and heard her say, about all he'd driven out to discuss. From now on, with the sun finally gone and the beautiful night settling in on all sides with its fragrance and its softness, whatever ensued would be social, not otherwise. Channing was still, off-duty or not, a detective pursuing leads.

Later, as they strolled side-by-side out to where his car stood in quiet shadows, he asked why she'd felt impelled to make that offer to pay for Frank Ford's heart specialist.

She was reflective about it when she replied. 'Doctor Spence was not, as you've probably guessed by now, a man motivated by generosity in his dealings with people. Especially the people who worked for him. Mister Ford was putting Janie through the University. He also had the normal obligations. He'd never have been able to afford that heart specialist.'

'That was generous of you,' murmured Channing, pausing beside the car to stand and look at her. Since the death of her husband only a month earlier, she had changed noticeably. He thought it was probably because now, at long last, she was an independent woman, wealthy, secure, untroubled. Then she said something that upset that little analysis somewhat.

'What of Thomas Engels, Inspector?'

'Nothing yet, although I have enough to take the case to the District Attorney for prosecution.'

'And you will do that?'

Channing inclined his head. 'Extortionists don't appeal to me very much, Mrs Spence.'

She nodded, so evidently they didn't appeal very strongly to her either, but she looked away for a moment and Channing thought she might be a little sad, too.

He said, 'Engels is lucky. It could have been suspicion of murder instead of just extortion.' He did not mention Attorney Greenspan's offer to trade. He did not expect that to come to anything.

Finally she turned back and said, 'I'll tell you something, Inspector, that doesn't have much bearing on what happened to my husband: He was a different man after marriage than he'd been before.'

Channing opened the car door, stepped in and leaned, looking up at her. 'Most men are, Mrs Spence. I'd have thought you'd have guessed that by now.' To take some of the sting from those words he also said, 'It's never a woman's fault, I don't suppose, but they are very poor judges of men. Always.'

He left her and drove slowly back through the lingering twilight to his flat, thinking some very unpolicemanlike thoughts, but being a detective did not preclude the possibility that a man was also just exactly that — a man.

18

Channing Starts the Final Countdown

Joe Barthelmess was absorbed in the backtracking of everyone in the Spence murder case who might not have a very valid alibi for the night of the murder, and excepting Mrs Spence's former husband, Engels, Joe was having to do some ferreting in almost each instance. John Harding, for example, who lived in the garage annexe alone, could very easily have been the murderer. At least he would have had a devil of a time proving that he hadn't been alone that night, watching television, as he claimed.

Inspector Channing didn't interrupt. In fact, after looking in on Barthelmess first thing in the morning, he drove over to Westwood, found an acceptable parking slot for a change, then waited in Gerald Wheaton's tiny office until Wheaton's current class was over and then they sat and idly talked for a while, after the manner of a pair of seasoned, unflappable detectives to whom the seamy and sordid side of life was all too familiar, and also, as detectives talked who never let any of the dirt rub off on them.

Actually, Channing wanted to intercept Janie Ford, so when he was fairly certain she would be along, he left Wheaton and went ambling down the main broadwalk where there were a number of green benches, designed for eye-appeal evidently rather than physical comfort, because the one Channing took, in pleasant tree shade beside the walkway, had his back aching within five minutes.

He shifted position, finally discovered a way to compromise between bench and back, then smoked a cigarette while he studied the faces of students moving past in both directions. Mostly, those faces were young and open and fresh. Now and then some older person went past, and also now and then he saw men who had to be instructors.

It was an interesting scene to someone like Inspector Channing to whom people, in their endless variety, were a pageant of not just race and shading, but of the historic and continuing march of Mankind.

Then Janie came along and he watched her before she saw him unobtrusively sitting in dark shade. She was very pretty this particular morning, eyes alive, cheeks bright with health, her stride firm and supple, her carriage, despite the loose clothing, erect and confident. He had to smile; how many body-blows did life give older people before they finally adopted the shuffling gait, the half-protective crouch, that came with middle age?

'Janie?'

She looked startled at sight of him, but she dutifully veered over to the bench and two stalwart youths, probably athletes, who had been following, looked at one another, shrugged, and kept on walking.

'Inspector.' She had a question in her eyes when he smiled and patted the bench for her to sit down. 'Is this how you spend your days off, Inspector, watching people?'

'Only the pretty ones, Janie.'

They could relax with each other. After all, they had shared some bad moments the night they'd met at the clinic after her father's heart attack. She sat sideways though, so she could study his face, so, relaxed though she might look and act, there was still a firm question in her attitude towards him.

'I need a little information,' he said, speaking softly and carefully. He wanted to be very careful now. 'Where did your parents live when your mother was alive?'

That baffled her, obviously, but she answered, giving the street name and the address of the house. Before she could ask why he wanted this information he eased in another question.

'And when your father went to work for Doctor Spence managing the buildings, and you saw the two of them together, did they act as though they were old friends?'

Janie's brows dropped a notch, evidently less in an effort to recall something than in an effort to understand what might lie behind the questions. 'I wouldn't describe them as old friends, Inspector. Old acquaintances but hardly old friends. After all, Doctor Spence was a wealthy, prominent man, and he carried himself with most people as though he didn't want anyone ever to forget that. With my father he was pleasant . . . sometimes a little patronizing, as though in giving my father his job he had been looking after a poor relation. But they did not seem to meet very often. Just their different schedules, I guess.'

Channing had a better definition. No man, Ford included, would willingly go where some stuffed-shirt like Carleton Spence, would deliberately slight him, especially in front of others — Janie, for example.

'Did they ever argue?'

Janie's brows dropped still another notch. 'No. I never heard them at it if they did. But I doubt that they had occasion to disagree. My father kept the books and managed the property without any difficulty. That would be the only reason they'd have to argue.'

'Not about you, Janie?'

Now the sensitive brows dropped like thunder. 'Inspector!'

Channing smiled and shook his head. 'Easy, Janie. I'm not hinting at that love-affair business at all. I believed you when you refuted the suggestion several weeks ago.'

'Then what *are* you driving at?'

'Well, Doctor Spence offered to foot the bill for you here at the University, and he wanted to help you arrange your academic schedule. Those things would be resented by the normal parent, I should think.'

Janie's face cleared at once. 'I'm sorry,' she murmured, then shook her head. 'My father listened when I told him of the offer to subsidize me. He simply said he'd done the job for twenty-one years, he'd go on doing it without outside help. As for the schedules, he even thought Doctor Spence had some good ideas. There was no friction there, Inspector.'

'About Doctor Linden, Janie . . . '

She sighed, set some books down

upon the bench and gazed tolerantly at Channing. 'My father thought Will was very nice. He said he thought he'd make me a good husband, and that Will had a promising future. He and Will got along famously.'

'Doctor Spence?' murmured Channing.

'Well, as you know, he didn't like the idea of me marrying Will. He never came right out and said very much. What could be said? After all, even if I weren't of age, Doctor Spence was simply my father's employer, he was nothing to me except a friend.'

'Did he antagonize Doctor Linden, that you know of?'

She shook her head, then frowned very slightly. 'Will is an intense person. He feels things more deeply than anyone I've ever known He was waiting for Doctor Spence to say something about disapproving of us seeing so much of each other. He told me he'd straighten Doctor Spence out the moment anything was said. It was my idea not to make an issue of it; that Will needed the job at the clinic and we weren't going to be married until I graduated anyway, so there was no real reason to get upset.'

Channing nodded. He hadn't expected more than he'd got, and as a matter of fact he hadn't actually meant to spend as much time as he had spent. But it was pleasant there, in the cool shade with Janie, and what was evolving in his mind was a lot less pleasant. In fact, if it turned out to be as he was beginning to fear it might, he wasn't looking forward to it at all.

After he offered to drive her home and she declined because she was going directly to the clinic instead, Channing drove to the offices of the lawyers who had served Doctor Spence while he'd been alive.

The senior member of that law firm, a greying, affable, keen-eyed man named Pierson, got a photostatic copy of the somewhat unusual Spence Will for Channing to peruse. Afterwards, with a fragrant cigar lighted, Pierson went over the long relationship he'd had with Doctor Spence.

Pierson's choice of words was careful,

always noncommittal, never offensive in any way, but to Inspector Channing, whose lifelong study had been people, their moods, attitudes and actions, the impression came across that Pierson, like so many others, had never actually held Doctor Spence in very high esteem.

'As for the Will,' said the lawyer, 'it's quite legal and acceptable. Sometimes people act like that — very secretive about their personal affairs. I'm used to it, Inspector, so if Spence chose to send in a sealed envelope with a handwritten Last Testament, it was fine with me.'

'Was Doctor Spence normally secretive, Mister Pierson?'

The lawyer considered the question carefully before replying. 'Well, he didn't give that impression, Inspector, and I knew him for a good many years, but only as a client. He did, on the other hand, seem to be different after his marriage.'

'Different in what way?'

'Oh, originally he asked us to draw up a Will leaving everything to the new Mrs Spence.'

Channing sat perfectly still, watching Pierson. When the lawyer pressed fingertips together and peered over them rather owlishly, Channing said, 'Why did he change it?'

'I have no idea. As I've said, one day we received the handwritten Will, which by law, since it bore a later date, superseded the Will my firm had drawn up for Doctor Spence.'

'How else did he seem changed?' Channing asked.

Pierson increased the pressure on his fingertips and studied them as he offered a delayed reply. 'The last time he was here, he mentioned a Doctor Linden — the same man, I presume, that was mentioned in the newspapers after the slaying, who worked at the clinic with Doctor Spence. All he said was something about young Linden getting a bit out of character, and insinuating himself into Spence's personal affairs.'

Channing said, 'Did he mention any names in connection with that remark; perhaps the name Maude, or the name Janie?'

'I'm sorry, Inspector, that's all Spence said, and I didn't want to get involved so I asked no questions. You know how it is in your work. Well, it's the same in mine. If you look or act sympathetic people bear down your shoulder with all their troubles. Doctor Spence was just one of our clients.'

Channing departed from the law offices shortly after this, looked at his watch, and decided to try and squeeze in one more interview before it was too late.

He almost didn't make it, at that, because although he had the address Janie had given him, not being familiar with the part of the city it was located in, he wasted a good deal of time just driving back and forth, searching.

And after that, although he had anticipated this, he wasted more time by trying to find someone in the nearby neighbourhood who might be able to recall residents who hadn't lived there in something like two decades. That in itself should have been a prohibitively difficult undertaking in a part of the world where people seldom lived longer than six or eight years in one area, but newspaper coverage of the Spence murder turned out to be a valuable aid.

The man he found was elderly, thin, stooped and predatory. He operated a grocery store on the intersection where the Ford's had lived, and the moment Channing mentioned who he was and what he wanted, the old grocer brightened noticeably.

'I been wonderin',' he said, 'how long it'd be before some of you people begun lookin' into the background of them people. Why, I remember the Fords like it was only yesterday. He was a tall, thin feller, quiet and mousy. His wife was a fine figure of a woman; wavy hair the colour of fresh honey, pretty as a picture. But she didn't get very friendly. Oh, they paid their bills right on the first of the month, good customers and all that, but I knew . . . In this business you get so's you can tell about folks. Now the little girl, she had a sweet way about her. Not sassy nor smart the way children are nowadays. You wouldn't believe my loss from petit theft, Inspector Banning.'

'Channing.'

'Yes. Well sir, the man and woman was a fine lookin' couple, but if there was any strength in 'em it had to be in the woman. And the little girl was a spittin' image of her, except that the little girl smiled and laughed and . . . '

It went on for a full hour before Channing could disentangle himself and get back to the car, without learning anything that might help. By then it was turning dusky off in the east and he was hungry. He thought of returning to the office to check with Joe, but that grocer had just about worn his nerves to the raw, so he instead ate on his way home and reached his flat just as darkness came down.

19

Some Enlightening Answers

Barthelmess had been at the office and was gone by the time Inspector Channing reached the place the next morning. Joe had left a note, but all it said was that he would get in touch with Channing when he returned.

It didn't matter very much. Channing drove out to the clinic and met Doctor Linden, who said something about Channing being out rather early. It was one of those ordinary things people said; Channing was invariably early, and actually by the time he reached the clinic it was nearly nine o'clock.

Linden took him into the office where a coffee urn was fragrantly sitting on a hot-plate. As Linden got two cups and filled them he talked, and the reason for his cheerfulness this morning was evidently the swift and steady recovery of Janie's father.

Linden told of Janie's visit the afternoon before, stating that her father had smiled for the first time since his heart attack. Channing was properly jubilant right along with Will Linden, then he asked if he might see the patient and Doctor Linden didn't even hesitate.

'Come along.'

The room where Frank Ford lay was at the rear of the building where noise would be minimized. It was a single, private room, the most expensive kind, incidentally, in a private sanitarium, or for the matter of that in any hospital.

It had off-white walls, a creamy ceiling, a monitoring intercommunication system built into the wall, and one window, the one facing the convalescent-yard was open admitting the scent of flowers and cool morning air.

Ford had great bluish circles beneath his eyes, he had lost weight again, so that now he looked more cadaverous than ever, and although his gaze was bright enough, it also had a fatalistic shadow to it.

Ford knew Inspector Channing and

nodded at him without smiling. Doctor Linden went to the bedside and felt Ford's wrist. He said, 'Inspector Channing was interested in your recovery, Frank.'

Ford nodded. He seemed strong enough and despite the splotchy, bad colouring, appeared quite fit and able. He sounded faintly funereal when he spoke, but then Inspector Channing had hardly expected him to emulate a foghorn.

'Do you have your murderer yet, Inspector?' Ford asked.

Channing smiled and wagged his head. 'Not yet, Mister Ford.'

The sick man nodded softly. 'Inspector, when a man was as close to it as I was, he begins to question a lot of things he's accepted all his life. I'm sure that in time you'll get your criminal, Inspector, but that saying — of the dead speak no evil — Inspector, I don't think that's such good advice.'

'Meaning, Mister Ford?'

'Carleton Spence was a first-class fraud, a cheat and a phony.'

Doctor Linden was startled but Channing's only reaction to those virulent words was to cross one leg over the other one and to examine a light scuff mark on the toe of one shoe.

Ford went on. 'I realize the law makes no distinction, Inspector. A murderer is a murderer regardless of what his victim may have been, and as I said, I'm confident you'll get your criminal — but take it from someone who knew Spence, he deserved killing.'

Will Linden finally spoke. 'Frank, apart from getting yourself worked up, this isn't very pleasant conversation you're making.'

'Who said it had to be?' demanded Ford.

Channing rose, smoothed his coat and stepped to the door as though to depart. He said, 'Mister Ford, I don't dispute anything you've said. If it'll make you feel any more justified, I can tell you several other people thought exactly the same thing about Doctor Spence. But there's one small flaw in your logic about his killing: suppose each individual were allowed to take the law into their own hands; suppose each of us could condemn to death one person we didn't like. Overnight one half the population of the world would die. Over a fortnight I suppose the other half would be pretty well decimated.'

Ford raised a blue-veined hand. 'I know each argument you can offer, Inspector, and for you each one is correct exactly as for me my own arguments are perfectly reasonable.'

When Doctor Linden joined Inspector Channing out in the cool, silent corridor he shook his head. 'He shouldn't upset himself.' Linden paced along, head down and looking unhappy, until they were back in his office, then he shot Channing a look from beneath lowered brows and said, 'Well, you have one man's opinion.'

'No, Doctor, not just one man's. I've heard it before, not always put quite so strongly, but only because the others were more circumspect.'

'Ford's a sick man, Inspector.'

Channing had never doubted it. 'But you have hopes for an eventual recovery?'

'Oh yes. Although I'm inclined to believe the poor devil has suffered

241

additional heart damage. Care for another cup of coffee?'

Channing declined, visited another few minutes with Doctor Linden, then left the clinic to drive over to the Spence estate, and this time, perhaps because it was a bit early for city-bound expeditioners to be gone, or perhaps because Maude Spence had no intention of going into Los Angeles that day, he caught her at home.

Harding was working in a stand of small trees and returned Channing's wave as the detective went on up to the front of the house and was admitted by Mary Martin, who smiled a little uncertainly at him, an attitude to which he was quite accustomed.

Maude was in the pantry and when she came to the front of the house to greet him she had her thick, wavy hair drawn back and held in place by a small green ribbon. She looked twenty instead of forty. She smiled and that made the impression even stronger.

'Coffee, Inspector Channing?'

He declined without explaining where

he'd already had a cup, then he followed her into the sitting-room and this time when they sat, Maude relaxed and said, 'I suppose solving a crime is somewhat like solving a jigsaw puzzle. Until you get all the pieces in place it's tantalizing.'

He nodded. That was a simile he'd heard before. It was fairly accurate too, except that it overlooked the fact that even detectives got weary after a while.

'I saw Frank Ford a while ago,' he said, watching her for reaction.

'I've meant to go over,' she murmured. 'Doctor Linden told me yesterday he'd be able to have visitors. How does he look?'

'I suppose, if he'd been robust before the seizure, he still wouldn't look exactly chipper, but as it is he looks fragile as glass to me.'

She nodded. 'He always impressed me as a sad man, Inspector.'

'Did you know him very well, Mrs Spence?'

'Not really. He'd come to the house, we'd politely discuss the weather, then he'd go into the study and be with my

243

husband — something to do with the buildings, book-keeping, things like that. I got to know his daughter fairly well, but Frank Ford always impressed me as a man no one, excepting Janie of course, could ever get very close to.'

Channing had got the same impression even before Ford's illness, but what he wanted to know now was just what, if anything, Mrs Spence knew of Ford's earlier connection with Carleton Spence.

'It seems to me your husband and Ford were fairly compatible,' he said. 'I suppose Doctor Spence felt Ford was a capable employee.'

She nodded. 'He said very little about him, although a time or two he did mention that Mister Ford was a good man. I suppose he meant Mister Ford managed the property well.'

'But they were not close, were they?'

Maude shook her head, 'No, I suppose they just didn't have very much in common.'

She made that statement easily and without any evident self-consciousness, which was precisely what Channing had been patiently waiting for. He rose saying he had to get back to his office; that he'd only dropped by because he'd been in the neighbourhood.

She went to the car with him as she'd done before, and as he climbed in she said, 'You remind me of a wise old grandfather, Inspector, and that's funny because you're nowhere nearly old enough for the part.'

He grinned up at her. 'Remember what I said, Mrs Spence; women don't make very good judges of men.'

'I remember it,' she assured him. 'I thought about it too, and you are so very right. It's too bad there's no way to tell young girls that simple truth, Inspector. It would prevent an awful lot of broken hearts.'

She was speaking of herself, as a young girl, obviously, but Channing chose not to let it show that he understood this. 'Well, you can always take Janie to one side, Mrs Spence.'

She quietly smiled down into his eyes. 'Would it do any good, Inspector?'

'Probably not; whoever heard of the

young taking advice from the old? Anyway, I think Doctor Linden will make a good husband for her. Don't you?'

He watched her eyes closely while awaiting her reply. There was nothing in their depths that would give him a clue that she had other thoughts about Doctor Linden, and that too was something he'd wanted to verify one way or another. Now, she gave him his answer, not so much in words as in attitude.

'I think so. Will is hard-working, dedicated, and definitely in love with Janie. Regardless of Doctor Spence's disapproval — and he *did* disapprove, you know — Janie and Will Linden are as well matched as two people can be. At least in my opinion, Inspector.' She smiled again. 'But as you've said, women aren't good judges of men.'

He left, wearing a soft smile. He'd got two worthwhile answers to things that had been bothering him slightly, and he'd also seen Maude Spence smile. If he didn't accomplish another thing for the balance of the day he'd feel satisfied.

He didn't, as a matter of fact,

accomplish much more, for when he finally walked into the office Joe was eating an apple hunched over the desk studying some sheets of paper. He looked up then stood up as though to relinquish desk and chair to its proper owner.

Channing waved him back down, tossed his hat aside and dropped into a chair out front of the desk. 'Anything?' he asked, and Barthelmess took an enormous bite from his apple then, with cheeks pouched like a chipmunk, shook his head.

'A hell of a lot of foot-work and nothing that we didn't already know or couldn't have guessed. By the way, Carter Spence called a while back.'

Channing groaned. 'Don't tell me — he's discovered a dark side to Carleton Spence; the doctor was a high-up official of the Mafia.'

Barthelmess laughed. 'You're getting cynical. That's a sign you need a holiday. Maybe a week of ocean fishing. No, Spence said he couldn't waste any more time down here, that his employers were screaming threats that if he didn't get

247

back up north they'd have to replace him. He's flying out this afternoon and left the telephone number of his hotel if we want to contact him before he leaves.'

Channing's gaze got ironic and amused. 'I think we can struggle along somehow without Mister Spence. At least I'm prepared to make the effort — and the sacrifice.'

Barthelmess finished his apple and lit a cigarette. 'Okay what have *you* come up with?'

Channing outlined the results of his mornings' work from the visit with Frank Ford to the discussion with Maude Spence. He pointed up nothing in particular until Joe asked about Maude's comments on Janie, then he also related the results of the discussion he'd had the afternoon before with that attorney named Pierson.

Barthelmess was interested in Pierson's opinion of both Spence and the hand-written Will. Channing said dryly, 'Pierson was very careful but I still got the impression he didn't like Doctor Spence.'

Barthelmess said, 'Who have you ever

talked to who did like him?'

'Well, not Frank Ford,' exclaimed Channing, and repeated a little of what the sick man had said.

Barthelmess blew smoke, looked at Channing and said, 'Anything to that stuff Carter Spence reported?'

Channing shook his head. Barthelmess meant the moonlight car-ride and the snatch of conversation Spence had heard. 'Not as far as I am concerned. And there's nothing going on between Maude Spence and Doctor Linden regardless of what young Spence seems to suspect.' Channing gazed at his watch. 'Did that apple fill you up or shall we go and get some lunch?'

Barthelmess pushed aside his notes and rose. He was ready to go, even though it was a half hour before high noon.

20

The Day Before Disclosure

Tommy Engels and his attorney were in the office with Channing the following morning when Joe Barthelmess arrived, but they'd only just got there so after everyone had nodded they went right on with what had brought them, Greenspan saying, 'Inspector, there's no point in trying to make a big extortion case out of what you have against Tommy. He didn't get a red cent from Mrs Spence. You only have her word for the fact that extortion was even likely.'

'Not quite,' said Channing mildly. 'Engels has a record; a reputation for things like this.'

Greenspan spread his hands. 'Prove it.'

Channing was just as direct. 'I don't have to prove it. That's up to the District Attorney once I hand over my evidence, and after that it'll be up to you to prove otherwise.' Channing smiled gently. 'Don't tell me a man can't be tried for his reputation.'

'He can't,' averred the lawyer and Channing kept right on smiling at the man.

'Of course he can't. But you'll have to explain that to a jury that's been reading of Tommy Engels skirmishes with the law for twenty years.'

Greenspan was even prepared for that. 'We'll simply ask for a change of venue.'

Channing looked at Joe Barthelmess who was standing over by the door looking on without comment. Channing looked bored. 'Good idea, Mister Greenspan,' he said, drifting his gaze back to the attorney again, but without the smile. 'Is there anything else?'

Engels spoke. He was very earnest. He even leaned in the chair as he said, 'Look, Inspector, it's only Maude's word that I tried anything.'

'That's good enough for me,' said Channing, and Tommy Engels hung on the edge of his chair a moment staring, before he spoke again.

'Inspector, in case you didn't know it, my ex-wife is no angel.'

Channing sat still returning Engels's stare. Greenspan and Joe Barthelmess were watching. Eventually, Channing rose, went silently to the door and opened it. 'Get out,' he said to Engels. Then he looked hard at Greenspan. 'Unless it has to do with Doctor Spence's murder or some other police matter, don't bring him around here again. Now get out both of you.'

The visitors rose, very conscious of having made a serious mistake, and as they passed through the doorway starting down the hall beyond, Greenspan said within Joe Barthelmess's hearing: 'Tommy, you've got a damned big mouth!'

Barthelmess closed the door, studied Channing a moment then went over to the window and quietly gazed down into the morning where city-life was beginning to weave its daylong patterns. When he turned back Channing was picking up the telephone. He called the Hall of

Records at Los Angeles' Civic Centre, got a crisp clerk and identified himself. He then asked if it would be possible to have a file-search instituted. The clerk snapped back that there just was not a large enough staff to do that, so Channing rang off, swivelled around and gazed at Joe.

Barthelmess grinned crookedly. 'Okay, what am I going down there to dig up?'

'The marriage licence of Janie's parents, the Fords. A copy of Janie's birth certificate, and to make it really thrilling for you, Joe, a copy of Mrs Spence's divorce from Tommy Engels.'

Barthelmess continued to gaze at Channing. 'You're onto something,' he said, half accusing Channing of withholding information.

'I'm onto a strong hunch, Joe. I've had it for a week now and I suppose it's time to start gathering in the evidence.'

Barthelmess waited a moment as though expecting Channing to say more, but when the silence had run on Joe reached for his hat. 'Big secret,' he growled, and Channing smiled.

'Not really. When you get back this afternoon I ought to have a few other loose ends tied up. I'll lay it all out for you then.'

Barthelmess had to be satisfied with that.

When Channing was alone he had a smoke standing by the same window Joe had recently gazed out of, then he went ambling off downstairs and out into what promised to be a hot, sticky day, and headed for the nearest coffee shop.

He actually didn't have much work to do, but he needed a little period of uninterrupted quiet to sort out some thoughts. He knew who had murdered Doctor Spence and he was satisfied why it had been done although he couldn't have offered one shred of physical proof.

But those things, he was confident, were about to be taken care of. What stumped him altogether was *how* the crime had been committed. He had an inkling but that was all, and even that inkling was pretty shaky.

On the way back to the office he met Fogarty, the laboratory technician, entering the building from the parking area. Fogarty greeted Channing, then said, 'It's going to be a scorcher today, Inspector.'

Channing nodded dutifully. One was never supposed to dispute any such statement. He fell in beside Fogarty and followed him halfway to the laboratory before saying he'd pick up that pacemaker and return it to the clinic. Fogarty was perfectly agreeable. He'd put the thing in a small box on top of a file cabinet. As he brought it over and handed it to Channing he said, 'That Ford who wore it, still alive?'

Channing nodded. 'They've got him wired up again.' He and Fogarty exchanged a smile, then Channing hiked on up to his office with the pacemaker, put it on his desk and reached for the telephone. He got the clinic on the second ring and was lucky enough to also get Will Linden.

'If you're going to be out there I'll bring back the pacemaker,' he told the medical man, and Linden confirmed what Channing already knew, that he would be on the clinic grounds somewhere all day long. But he also had another bit of relevant information to impart.

'I hired another physician yesterday afternoon, so it looks as though I may have a little respite now, after all.'

Channing did not leave the office right away. He instead ambled back down to the laboratory and had a brisk little conversation with Fogarty again. It was after this that he took the pacemaker out to his car, still in its little box, and drove down towards the ocean.

But instead of going to the clinic he drove to the house on Sixteenth Street, and whether he expected to or not, found Janie at home.

She greeted him quizzically, led him into the parlour and when he made easy conversation by utilising what he knew would be of interest to her — Will Linden's hired helper — she lost some of her curiosity about this visit and smilingly said that she and Will had decided not to wait until she graduated from the University to be married, and planned now to do it within the next few weeks.

Channing congratulated her. He meant

what he said. He liked Janie and he thought Doctor Linden, although somewhat narrow, was probably very good husband-material. Then he asked if they shared similar hobbies and she told him of surfing with Will Linden, or scuba-diving with him.

'Wasn't your father a little worried about sports like that?' he asked.

She laughed. 'Dad thought they were great. Now and then he'd go to the beach with us. Of course his condition prevented him from taking any part, but he perfected an improved flutter-valve for our air tanks.'

Channing was interested. 'I had no idea he was a machinist.'

Janie played it down, 'Actually, Dad was a tinkerer. He had a little shop out in the garage — the other half of the garage which he boarded up. That's where he improved on the flutter-valves. He also worked on improving the pacemaker for heart patients.'

Channing said, 'I'd like to see that. I had no idea he was anything more than a book-keeper.'

Janie's answer showed quiet pride. 'Dad actually was more than a tinkerer. I only said that because he worked in his shop off and on. He never tried to patent anything or even to market some of the things he created. But I remember the time he built a drying attachment that fitted on to ordinary washing machines. It was really quite good.' Janie grinned impishly. 'But the first time he tried it I came home and found him down on his hands and knees mopping water like mad. Later though, he made the thing fully automatic. As soon as the washing machine had gone through its spin-dry cycle, Father's device took over with a heat cycle of its own. Within ten minutes it had washed clothes dry enough for immediate ironing.'

'Sounds very spectacular,' said Channing. 'Why didn't he do anything with it?'

Janie simply shrugged. 'It's still out in the shop. I asked him the same question. He'd just say maybe someday.'

'I'd like to see it.'

Janie was apologetic. 'I don't know

where he keeps the shop keys, Inspector. When he comes home I'll get him to show it to you.'

Channing stayed a little longer, then made his exit. If it ever occurred to Janie that he'd never stated the reason for his visit, he was at the clinic, probably, before she had occasion to wonder.

Will Linden was in his office. It was close enough to the end of the month, he explained, for statements to be prepared for mailing out. He had an Administrative Receptionist who normally did this work, but as luck would have it she'd been taken ill three days earlier leaving it all for Linden to do.

He confessed to an abhorrence for paperwork of any kind. He also confessed to having asked Janie to stop in at his office later in the afternoon when she came from the University to visit her father.

'I'll dragoon her into doing it for me.'

They laughed about that, then Channing handed over the pacemaker in its box. 'Nothing wrong with it,' he said. 'Our lab people include an expert on them. He said this one is perfectly reliable.'

Linden, for the first time since Channing had known him, avoided meeting Channing's gaze. He took the box, peered into it, then put the box upon a little occasional table and went back behind the desk again.

'Anything bothering you, Doctor?' asked Channing.

The intercom buzzer interrupted. Doctor Linden, then said, 'All right, but make certain that someone is in the garden with him.' He flicked the intercom switch and wagged his head. 'They get cantankerous sometimes. This is a particular patient, an elderly man, who has dominated everyone all his life and even though I've told him he shouldn't exert himself too much, he still insists on going out into the convalescent garden.' Linden made a wry smile. 'Maybe I should have specialized in obstetrics.'

Channing chuckled. 'As little as I know of both specialties I believe I'd prefer geriatrics; at least you don't have emotional mothers to deal with.'

Linden appreciated that remark, leaned back and said, 'You're right, Inspector.' Then, after a moment when they appraised one another, he also said, 'Yes, something is bothering me. Frank Ford.'

'Given up?'

'What made you say that?' Linden asked, surprised.

'Yesterday, the way he talked and looked, made the idea cross my mind.'

'Well, you're perfectly right. And I don't understand it. He's not in any particular pain, I see to that. And Janie, about the only thing he still loves, comes by every day. In fact, I'd say that's all he lives for. Otherwise, each day he acts more and more like he's slipping into the vegetable state — lives, breathes, eats, understands, but does not willingly respond at all.'

Channing lit a smoke, considered the ashtray Linden pushed across towards him, and said, 'The death-wish, Doctor?'

Linden didn't like either that layman's term nor its implication in this particular case. He said, 'There has to be a very substantial reason for your so-called death-wish, Inspector. Frank Ford lacks it. In fact, he should be in moderately high spirits. After all, as I just said, he has a beautiful and delightful daughter. And of course he is alive when by all rights he might not have been.'

Channing rose. 'It was just something I read one time, Doctor. Well; I've got to get back to the office. I'm expecting some papers to arrive.'

Linden went as far as the reception desk with Channing. There, they parted easily and Channing went thoughtfully out to his car, heaved a big sigh, climbed in through layers of heat, and began to drive back to police headquarters.

21

Channing Goes Housebreaking

Carter Spence dropped by Channing's office on his way to the Municipal Airport, interrupting Channing at his job of writing a report for the District Attorney's office on Engels's extortion attempt.

Spence was entitled to know what progress had been made towards finding his uncle's killer — up to a point, of course — and Inspector Channing told him about such things as Tommy Engels, Doctor Spence's meddling in Janie Ford's life, some of the other sidelights. But Carter Spence was no fool. He wanted to know what specific progress had been made towards revealing the murderer, and Channing had no intention whatever of going that far in disseminating information.

But Channing did say, 'I think we'll be

writing you shortly, giving full particulars.'

That seemed to surprise Spence. Not that the case might be resolved shortly, but that Channing would write him when it was. He commented, and Channing's reply was simple. He said he'd developed the technique of writing letters of this kind to involved people years ago, so that no one was left wondering. He called it 'good public relations,' and laughed.

Carter Spence departed after a firm handclasp, and promised, if Channing ever came to his part of British Columbia, to show him some great hunting. Channing smiled until he'd closed the office door. If there was one participation sport he didn't care for, it was hunting!

He got back to the report on Thomas Engels. He had no deposition from Mrs Spence, nor under ordinary circumstances would he have taken one. That was part of the District Attorney's job.

Frequently, though, policemen *did* get statements, which were sent along with their reports, and in some places District Attorneys demanded such statements, preferring them as the basis for criminal prosecution.

In Channing's case no such demand had ever been made, not entirely because there was such excellent co-operation and esteem between the office of the District Attorney and the police department — that was very rarely ever the case — but because the District Attorney had his own Special Investigators who were always, without exception, sent forth to investigate each case submitted to him for prosecution. These men were usually better trained in law than the average detective. They had to be if a District Attorney was not to end up trying cases in court in which he was constantly being defeated.

Notwithstanding, Channing sat at his desk, pen poised, turning over in his mind whether or not he should drive out to the Spence estate. Of course he didn't have to; the District Attorney's men would take over as soon as his report reached them, but there was no getting around it, Channing liked the company of Maude Spence.

He didn't make the trip, however, because mid-way through the silent argument with himself the telephone rang. It was Doctor Spence's attorney Pierson calling to ask if the police had any pending charge against Maude Spence because Pierson's office was going ahead with the probating of the Will, which would otherwise not be expedited pending the outcome of any police action.

Channing said there was no charge pending; that as far as he knew now there would be no charge made. He did not mention any other suspect and Pierson did not ask about anyone but Mrs Spence, but he did say he'd had another discussion with Carter Spence, and that the nephew was of the opinion now, that a total stranger had slipped into the house and had killed his uncle while being caught in the act of burglarizing the place.

Channing groaned inwardly, but if Pierson was using that as a means for prying out some information, he had the wrong man. Channing merely said, 'I think that's improbable. I wouldn't rule it out altogether, but I think it's not very probable.'

By the time he got rid of Pierson he didn't have a whole lot of time left to finish the report on Engels. But a benign fate intervened on his behalf permitting the ultimate completion. He then left the office, taking the report in person to its destination. It was common practice.

Except for that he might have got the telephone call Joe Barthelmess excitedly made from Civic Centre. As it was the call was intercepted by one of the typing-pool secretaries to whom Joe had nothing to say since his message was of interest only to Channing personally.

The girl made a face at the telephone as she put it upon its stand, scribbled a note saying only that Barthelmess had called, and sauntered to Channing's office to place it on top of the desk. If regulations hadn't required it, she wouldn't even have made a note, because Barthelmess hadn't actually said anything.

He would have, if he'd got hold of Channing, but that contact was not made. Barthelmess was frustrated, Channing was over at the District Attorney's office, and the day was moving along towards its ultimate ending.

Fogarty, the laboratory technician, returned those mud castings of an alleged murderer's shoe imprints to Channing's office. Both casts were carefully boxed and cushioned in wadded-up newspaper. The report was stapled to the box. It said nothing Channing hadn't already elicited.

However, there was a second note — with different file numbers neatly typed in the upper right-hand corner — belated but nonetheless valid, saying that in the experienced judgement of the specialist in the laboratory section, that pacemaker which had been submitted for study, had been forcibly removed from the person who had been wearing it.

Even that scrap of information, surprising as it might have been in most sectors, would not have brought Channing up short in astonishment, and by now, knowing what Barthelmess had to have figured out down there at the Hall of Records, coupled with what he already knew of the Spence murder case, it would not have startled Barthelmess very much either.

Channing went over his report with an acquaintance, one of the District Attorney's Special Investigators, afterwards had a pleasant little visit over a smoke, then returned to the office, managing to reach there exactly three minutes after Barthelmess had tried one last time to reach him.

This time the note the girl left said simply that Barthelmess was going home from Civic Centre, since it was closer, and that he would therefore not see Channing until the next morning.

It didn't matter. Barthelmess might be excited over what he'd dug up, but Channing, who already thought he knew what the records would disclose, was quite capable of waiting another day — or another week for the matter of that. No one could ever accuse Inspector Channing of being an impatient person. Calmly, almost irritatingly thorough, but always in a manner that was almost gentle.

He had one unexpected visitor when he got back. Janie Ford came by and seemed relieved to find Channing alone. She had been contacted by Doctor Spence's solicitors who were interested in knowing what action she proposed taking with respect to legal representation.

Channing had to smile. Pierson, for all his low-key attitude and unmistakable affluence, was not one to let grass grow underfoot; clients with readymade incomes were worth cultivating.

Channing said non-committally he thought Pierson would probably be a very good lawyer. Janie agreed. She said she had tentatively agreed for that law firm to handle the legal angles of the inheritance for her.

'Their fees are shocking,' she told Channing.

His answer was pithy. 'Well, I've heard of very few professional people — doctors *or* lawyers — who work entirely out of dedication to the human weal.'

Janie said, 'My father has been writing little notes about the property, when he's up to it, and when he thinks of something

I ought to know, as owner.' She stopped speaking and looked steadily at Inspector Channing for a moment, then said, 'Do you think I ought not to accept Doctor Spence's property?'

Channing sat behind his desk gazing at her. She was very pretty. Young, of course, which was too bad, and woefully inexperienced, which would be awfully annoying to an older man, and dreadfully naïve. He said, 'Really, Janie, it's not my position to advise you. Doctor Linden should do that. Or your father.'

'It was one of the notes my father wrote that had me stop by here today, Inspector.' She fished it out of a voluminous leather purse and handed it to him. It said simply and succinctly: 'Janie, if you need mature judgement, go and see Inspector Channing.'

He handed the note back and sat thoughtfully regarding his guest. Then he shook his head. 'Look, Janie, Doctor Spence wanted you to have those buildings. I don't even know the extent of them nor their worth, but *he* did, and it was his wish you should have them. My advice

271

would be for you to keep them. Anyway, what else could you do — there's no way to hand them back.'

Janie said, 'I was thinking of Mrs Spence, Inspector Channing.'

He nodded. 'Why don't you go by and ask her what she thinks?'

'Yes, I could do that couldn't I?' Janie rose smiling. 'You're very nice, Inspector,' she said, then added a qualifying: 'Sometimes.'

After she'd gone Channing reached for the telephone, dialled the Spence estate and asked for Mrs Spence. Before she came to the telephone he lit a smoke, cocked back his chair and planted both feet atop the desk.

He told her about Janie's visit, asked what she thought Janie ought to do, and got back just about the answer he'd been fishing for.

'I don't think there's any doubt, Inspector. My husband wanted her to have the properties. That's very clear. It doesn't seem to me I should take them even though she offered them. Does it seem that way to you?'

'Well, as you know very well, none of this has anything to do with me. In fact, I'm forbidden by regulations from becoming involved at all. But I thought I knew what your answer would be, which is why I asked her to stop by and see you. Furthermore, there is one more thing — but I'd prefer telling you that personally, and only when I'm absolutely sure of myself.'

Maude Spence said, 'It sounds solemn, and mysterious.'

Channing, declining to be drawn out, said, 'If I can, I'd like to drop by tomorrow morning, sometime before noon.'

'I'll be right here waiting, Inspector,' she said.

Afterwards, Channing replaced the telephone, studied his watch, stepped to the window to also study the dusky sky, then he went quietly and purposefully down to his car in the parking area. The last thing Janie had said, from the doorway as she was leaving, was that she'd have to hurry with her visit to Maude because she and Doctor Linden were going out to supper this evening.

Channing checked the glove-compartment of his car for the leather case he'd tossed in there earlier. He also listened to the unfriendly sounds his stomach was making. He'd had no dinner and it was past time.

Then he drove out of the parking area heading in the opposite direction from his flat, and felt the wonderful coolness as nightfall came closer and as daylight retreated down behind the farthest horizon.

He didn't drive home and he veered off where he could have taken the route to Spence's clinic. Neither did he take the road leading to the Moorish hilltop estate of the late Doctor Spence.

He drove casually, allowing plenty of time, and when he cruised past the house on Sixteenth Street, finally, only the porch light was burning, all the rest of the place was dark, and obviously no one was there.

Still, he drove round the square until he found a small cafe, and there he ate a leisurely meal before returning to the

Sixteenth Street address.

Finally, parking down a few doors, he took the little leather case from the glove-compartment, pocketed it, left his hat in the car, alighted and walked back.

He went directly up the driveway, pausing only once to ascertain that in fact Janie was indeed gone, he had the entire place to himself, then he went to the locked workshop round back, dug out the leather case and with infinite patience began trying master-keys until he found one that would unlock the door.

Somewhere, a few doors away, someone slammed a door. Channing stood a moment waiting to see whether this would have any bearing upon what he was up to, and when it did not seem to, he stepped inside the little shop, very carefully closed the door first, then switched on the overhead lights.

The place looked like it belonged to a man who, when he came here at all, never did so with any thought in mind of being very tidy. But it also appeared to be well furnished with a lathe, punch-press, router, even an electric forge.

22

The Last Death

The following morning Detective Inspector Channing and Detective Joe Barthelmess drove to the clinic. It was one of those pastel mornings when dawn lingers on into the later time of day.

Doctor Linden was there. So was Janie Ford as well as Maude Spence. They were there by prearrangement and upon the entrance of the policemen Doctor Linden left his desk-chair to get two more cups of coffee from the hot-plate in his office.

It was good coffee, which surprised Channing, a bachelor who'd been making coffee many years and who still had not mastered the art of it.

Barthelmess set aside what looked to be a rolled-up bit of carpeting, perhaps a hall-runner or the like. Channing commented on the coffee and Maude

Spence, who was watching him, took a sip from her own cup evidently to see what was so excellent.

Channing got the rolled-up object Barthelmess had set against the wall, removed the covering and put the thing on Doctor Linden's desk.

'That is the very powerful man who rammed the knife into Doctor Spence.'

'It looks like a fat spyglass,' said Janie. 'I don't understand.'

Channing and Barthelmess, still solemn as judges, were prepared for that question, as inevitably they would have been. Joe opened the window overlooking the convalescent garden — empty this early in the day — and Inspector Channing took the fat tube over there, aimed at the ground and suddenly a great knife flashed soundlessly to half bury itself out there in the turf.

Doctor Linden's exclamation was for them all. 'Good Lord!'

Channing left Joe to retrieve the buried knife and put the cylinder from which it had been ejected back on top of the desk. 'Ingenious,' he said. 'Not particularly so in principle — soundless mechanical propulsion; people have been doing something like that since the crossbow — but this thing is ingenious because the man who designed and made it evidently did so in order to make a definite impression — and he succeeded at least for a while — that Doctor Spence's murderer was a virile, very strong person.'

Linden lit a cigarette and Channing noticed his hands were not very steady. Maude and Janie were watching Channing somewhat in the manner of birds watching a snake.

Joe Barthelmess was back with the knife, which he put beside the tube on Linden's desk. Joe had nothing at all to say. When Inspector Channing reached into a pocket and drew forth a little thick sheaf of papers, Joe looked even more reticent and solemn.

Channing said, 'I have here the photostatic copy of a marriage licence.' He detached it from the other papers and read off the names. One was Carleton Spence, the other name belonged to a woman no one in that room was the least bit familiar with. Channing looked at them all. 'That was Doctor Spence's first wife. As you all may know, she died several years later. What you may not know was that she was fairly wealthy.' Channing took out the next paper from the sheaf in his hand. 'I don't know that her wealth had anything to do with what I'm about to disclose to you now.'

Channing looked at the paper in his hand a moment, then silently handed it to Janie Ford. It was her birth certificate. While Janie was intently studying this document Channing told the others what he'd discovered.

'Doctor Spence, evidently at the same time he was courting the woman he married, was seeing Janie's mother. As the records show, he did not marry Janie's mother. Doctor Spence is dead, so we have to draw our own conclusions about that. At any rate, Janie was born — but her mother was not alone at the time. She was still unmarried and remained so for almost a year after Janie's birth, but she was not alone.'

'Then she married Frank Ford?' whispered Janie looking glassy-eyed at Inspector Channing, who nodded silently and held up the third sheet of paper, which was the copy of a marriage certificate.

Channing said softly, 'Now you know why Doctor Spence was so interested in your welfare, Janie. And why he was so protective towards you when it seemed you might get married. I think his feelings were not only genuine — I also believe he was very repentant for what he'd done over twenty years before. But there is one thing I don't know yet, although I expect to have that answer within the next few minutes.'

Maude slipped a hand over Janie Ford's fingers and exerted gentle pressure. The younger woman silently handed Maude the copy of the birth certificate. Janie was white but she had control of herself, which both Channing and Barthelmess saw with relief. They'd discussed the possibility of something different on the drive out and this actually was the only moment they had both dreaded.

Channing spoke again. The others sat watching him, and somewhere in the building a melodious gong sounded, which may have been summoning the ambulatory patients to the clinic's dining-room, although no one in Doctor Linden's office heeded the sound.

'The person who killed Doctor Spence was very well known to him. They had known each other for more years than either of them had known anyone in this room. That accounts for the ease with which the murderer got into the house unseen the night of the murder.'

Now, there wasn't a sound in the office. Nor even any movement. Janie and Maude's hand were still interlocked and now Maude was as pale as Janie also was. *They knew!*

'The murderer's reasons may have been simply the final outlet of lifelong pent-up hatred, although if this were so my guess is that something had to happen to bring it to a head that particular night. But we'll also have to get that answer in a few minutes. Right now we're concerned with the fact that the murderer got inside the house without difficulty, which is understandable. Doctor Spence of course had no idea he was slated to die. Afterwards, the killer got out of the house as simply as he'd got in — by simply walking out.

'Luck helped, only one person *might* have seen him enter — Mrs Spence — but she had something very crucial on her mind. She had no inkling the killer was even around. She was bent on trying to save Doctor Spence's reputation from her former husband, who also knew the truth about Janie and her parentage and was trying to blackmail her.

'Then, after committing murder, the killer of Doctor Spence had already made plans to take his own life. He very nearly succeeded. In fact, ironically enough, he was prevented from doing this by the very person he had avenged — his daughter.'

Doctor Linden suddenly blurted out a name: 'Frank. Good Lord, you're talking about Frank Ford!'

Channing nodded, then went on speaking. 'Waiting until he was sure he'd be unobserved and uninterrupted,

282

Mister Ford deliberately tried to break his pacemaker, the only insurance he had that his heart would continue to function. You all know what happened next: Janie found him, got him to the clinic, and Doctor Linden managed to keep him alive.'

The intercom buzzed on Linden's desk giving everyone a start. Linden crossed over swiftly, threw the little switch, listened briefly, then straightened up and hurried from the room without speaking. Channing threw Joe Barthelmess a look and Joe instantly went hastening out after the doctor.

Channing then pointed to the tube on the desk. 'Ford manufactured that thing in his workshop. Since it's not something anyone could make in a few hours, I'd say he'd made his plans several weeks in advance of the time he killed Doctor Spence with it. Which, under the law, proves premeditation, one of the essentials for prosecuting anyone for murder. I found that thing in his workshop last night.'

Channing sighed, took the last slip of

paper from the ones he was holding and held it up. 'This is a copy of Doctor Spence's handwritten Will. I'm only guessing now, but I think this may have been the cause of the dispute between Mister Ford and Doctor Spence. Ford demanded, since he had no idea how much longer he'd live — which meant he didn't know what would become of Janie after he died — or perhaps because he'd already planned to commit suicide, I don't know which, that Doctor Spence justify his wrongs of two decades ago by making certain Janie would be taken care of. Doctor Spence, probably out of remorse, not fear of threats, wrote this new Will and sent it to his attorneys. If he had told Ford what he'd done I think Doctor Spence would be alive today. Ironically, although in the end Doctor Spence did the right thing, he was too proud a man to admit it — so Frank Ford, believing he *hadn't* done it, killed him out of frustration and hatred.'

Channing pocketed the papers, lit a cigarette and went back to stand by the window as he said, 'Well, that's about it, ladies. I'm sorry, very sorry.' He turned to gaze out into the yard. 'Harding substantiated what I already suspected when he gave me some imprints of footprints, saying one of them belonged to the killer. Harding was wrong. None of them belonged to the murderer, but in a way that only confirmed the identity of the killer, because while everyone else had been to the house since the killing, only one man had not — and that was because he was right here in this hospital, unable to go to the house. It certainly wasn't enough to make an arrest upon, nor even enough to confront the killer with, but it was enough to make me want to make a thorough investigation of this suspect — and that is when I found the murder weapon.'

Channing turned and Doctor Linden and Joe Barthelmess came silently into the room, their faces grey and troubled.

Doctor Linden said, 'Well he succeeded this time.'

No one spoke as Linden walked wearily over behind the desk and dropped down. Channing gazed at Barthelmess, who very gently nodded his head.

'Frank Ford is dead,' announced Will Linden. 'And I think it proves your point, Inspector. This time he dislocated the new pacemaker, and this time, because his heart was already seriously weakened from his last seizure, it simply stopped.'

Janie turned, buried her head against Maude Spence's shoulder and wept silently. The men looked dumbly at one another. Channing jerked his head and led the way silently out into the yonder corridor where he, Joe Barthelmess and Will Linden stood gloomily together.

Channing said, 'There are loose ends, Doctor. In a way what Ford did is best all around, but we'll have to turn in our final report to the District Attorney.'

Linden looked up. 'What can he do?'

'Nothing,' answered Channing. 'He certainly can't prosecute. I'm not even sure he could have if Ford had lived — not successfully at any rate.'

Linden shook his head. 'Poor Frank. He had to love Janie very much.'

Channing could agree to that without reservation. 'Of course he did; after all, he raised her. I would guess he dedicated himself to that task because she was all he had left of the woman he loved so very much — Janie's mother. And it seems very probable to me that when Spence began to show an interest in his daughter, Ford was inflamed by that too.' Channing looked from Linden to Barthelmess, then said, 'There's a moral here somewhere, gentlemen, but I'm a policeman not a moralist.' He shoved out his hand and Doctor Linden shook it soberly.

'You've been a very unusual policeman, Inspector, and in time Janie will understand and appreciate that,' said Linden.

Channing disengaged his hand, smiled and started on down the cool, immaculate corridor. Joe Barthelmess walked after him. When they were outside in the beautiful morning with flower-scent in the air, Joe held the car door for Channing, then went to his side, got in and said, 'Ford knew, Bob. He *had* to know, otherwise he couldn't possibly have picked that very moment to die.'

Channing eased the car round and

headed for the roadway beyond. 'He knew, Joe, the only time I ever visited him back there. I was sure he knew that we were closing in on him from some of the things he told me that day.'

'It's better the way he did it, anyway.'

Channing didn't dispute that. In fact, he didn't say anything at all until they were back at headquarters in the parking area, then, as he alighted and took down a big breath of the fresh morning air, he said, 'Joe, that damned Doctor Spence had so much ego he couldn't even unbend enough to tell Ford he'd taken care of Janie's future. And that cost them both their lives.'

Barthelmess said, 'Well, maybe, Bob. But when I was in the room with Linden and Ford, the doctor, after making sure Ford was dead, said he couldn't have lived another six months anyway; that despite his apparent rapid recovery, his heart had been too badly damaged by this last seizure.'

They went on into the building, which was bustling with fresh activity for a new day, reached Channing's office, and there they had an hour to go over the case, but since it was closed now, and with a finality beyond earthly influence, the only thing left to discuss was the matter of Channing's initial suspicions. These were pretty well understood between them by now, so Joe Barthelmess finally left, and Channing, with the file on his desk, wrote only a few lines to the bottom of his report, then closed the file, which also closed the Doctor Spence murder case.

THE END

We do hope that you have enjoyed reading this large print book.

Did you know that all of our titles are available for purchase?

We publish a wide range of high quality large print books including:
Romances, Mysteries, Classics, General Fiction, Non Fiction and Westerns.

Special interest titles available in large print are:
The Little Oxford Dictionary Music Book, Song Book Hymn Book, Service Book

Also available from us courtesy of Oxford University Press:
Young Readers' Dictionary (large print edition) Young Readers' Thesaurus (large print edition)

For further information or a free brochure, please contact us at:
**Ulverscroft Large Print Books Ltd., The Green, Bradgate Road, Anstey, Leicester, LE7 7FU, England.
Tel:** (00 44) **0116 236 4325
Fax:** (00 44) **0116 234 0205**